THE INFINITELY OF ELLA AND MICHA

AND MICHA

(ELLA AND MICHA, #5)

JESSICA SORENSEN

The Infinitely of Ella and Micha

Jessica Sorensen

All rights reserved.

Copyright © 2020 by Jessica Sorensen

ISBN: 978-1939045560

For information: jessicasorensen.com
Cover design by MaelDesign

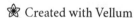 Created with Vellum

ELLA

MICHA and I are currently on the road, touring with bands. We haven't been married very long, but things have been fantastic so far. I wouldn't say perfect, because perfection doesn't exist. But I feel like this is pretty damn close to perfection.

Me being me, though, I worry that it could all be taken away from me at any given moment. I despise that my mind works that way, but there isn't much I can do about it. This is who I am, and now I just have to learn to live with that. And, as of right now, the possibility of that seems pretty good.

Content. That's the word that comes to mind as I lie in bed, stretched out across the mattress, wrapped up in a sheet. I have one of Micha's T-shirts on, the scent of him flooding my nostrils. I breathe it in, keeping my eyes shut, feeling super damn lazy, and in no way, shape, or form having any plans of moving. Well, I don't until I realize that I think I'm in the bed alone.

I roll over, opening my eyes and, yep, sure enough, the other half of the bed is empty.

Where in the heck is Micha?

I sit up, tucking a strand of my auburn hair behind my ear, blinking a few times to clear the sleepiness from my eyes. Then I peer around the quiet hotel room, wondering where on earth Micha is. The bathroom door is open, so I can tell he isn't in there.

Dragging my butt out of bed, I pad over to the curtains covering the glass doors that lead to the balcony, my head throbbing a little from a hangover.

As sunlight instantly blinds me, I shield my eyes with my hand until they stop burning. Then I lower my hand and glance out at the balcony, but Micha isn't there either.

I turn around and check the time. It's just past noon, which is too early for practice.

It isn't like him to take off like this. Not without waking me up first or leaving a note ...

A smile touches my lips as I spot the piece of paper sitting on the nightstand. I walk over, pick it up, and unfold it.

My Beautiful Wife (Can I just say how much I love the sound of that?),

Mike called me this morning and wanted to have a meeting. You looked so peaceful sleeping that I didn't want to wake you. I'm not sure how long I'll be gone, but I'll text you when I know. I'm hoping we can meet up and get something to eat before I have to head over to practice. If not, I'm going to try to stop by the room or wherever you end up today.

I love you, Ella May. You're the other half of my soul.

Micha

My smile expands a little as I fold up the note and walk over to my suitcase. Then I take out a little, wooden box, open it, and put the note in there with all the other ones he's written me. I love that he does that—writes me notes instead of texting me.

I'm still smiling like a lovestruck idiot as I put the box back into my suitcase and take out a black shirt, jeans, a bra, and a pair of panties. Then I head for the bathroom to get ready for the day.

I'm not sure what I'll do to fill up my time, since I'm ahead on my online classes, but I'll figure something out. We're in Phoenix, Arizona right now, and I've never been here before, so wandering around and sightseeing seems like a good option. I just wish Micha could go with me, but he's usually busy. Not that he doesn't make time to spend with me. We've been on the road for just over a month, and he spends every single extra minute he has with me, spoiling me, loving me. I'll admit, it's kind of strange—being loved. It's something I'm still getting used to, but I'm glad I gave myself the chance to.

By the time I get into the bathroom, a smile has consumed my face. It's a little strange to be so happy, but I roll with it, letting happiness take over me as I set my clothes down on the counter and move over to the shower to turn the water on. Then I strip out of Micha's T-shirt and step inside to wash up.

Last night, Micha and I went out to a bar with a couple of the other band members and got some drinks. It was a kind of a dive bar, and I can still smell the scent of alcohol.

I pull a face at the stench leaking off me then grab some shampoo and body wash and start scrubbing off the night. By the time I'm done, I smell like strawberries and vanilla, which makes me hungry, probably because I'm hungover.

I need something to eat, like now. Something greasy, like a burger.

Shutting off the water, I climb out of the shower, get dressed, dry my hair, and dab on some kohl eyeliner and lip gloss. Then I exit the bathroom and grab my phone off the nightstand to see if Micha has messaged me yet.

For the first time since I woke up, I frown.

No new messages, which means the meeting with Mike, his producer, is running long. I wonder why. Not that I think it's bad. Micha is an amazing singer, so I'm sure the meeting is a good thing. Still, I'm bummed out that I might not get to see him before he heads off to practice. The concert is tonight, though, so I'll be going to that. Right now, though, I'm starving, so I'm getting something to eat.

I dither on whether or not to just order room service then remember that I saw a little old-school café next door. It kind of reminded me of the diner back in Star Grove, my hometown.

I collect my keycard, some cash, and my phone, slip on a pair of clunky boots, and head out.

The hallway is empty as I make my way down it and to the elevators. Normally, the hotels Micha and I stay in are pretty average, but this place is much nicer, and it gave a discount to the tour. Not that Micha and I are totally broke, but his career hasn't taken off yet and I'm still working on my degree, so we have to live on a budget. Honestly, I'm not positive what I'll do once I graduate in a couple of years. I know I want to do something with art. Ideally, I'd like to be able to live off selling my artwork. In reality, that's probably not going to happen. Maybe I'll open an art gallery or something. Not that I have to decide right now. I have time to decide my future. The important part is that I'm choosing to have one.

By the time the elevator reaches the lobby, my belly is grumbling with hunger, so I hurriedly get off and make a beeline for the exit doors. However, I'm blindsided by a woman with short brown hair, wearing a black dress, a leather jacket, and square-framed glasses. She looks around my age, maybe a year or two older. I literally have no clue who she is, yet, with a huge smile on her face, she acts like she knows me.

"Hey!" she greets me as she steps in front of me and gives me a little wave. "You're Ella, Micha's wife, right?"

"Um … yeah?" It sounds more like a question, my confusion evident.

She laughs, her eyes crinkling around the corners. "You don't remember me, do you?"

I offer her an apologetic look as I shake my head. "Sorry."

She chuckles. "That's okay. I looked a bit different last night, because I was wearing extensions and contacts. Imagine me with long, brown hair and without the glasses."

It clicks then who she is. Well, sort of.

"Oh, you were at the bar last night, right?" While I can kind of make the connection, I can't remember her name. I'm blaming that on the shots I had, though. I do remember she's dating one of the bassists in the band.

"Yep. I'm Remi, just in case you forgot. We were all pretty trashed last night," she says. "It was fun, though."

"For sure," I agree, internally grimacing as my belly starts to grumble.

I don't want to be a total bitch, but I'm not much for socializing with people I barely know while I'm sober. That's more Tipsy Ella. Honestly, I'm not really one for socializing in general. The only people I really talk to are Lila, Ethan—well, I talk to Ethan mostly through Lila—my brother's wife, Caroline, on occasion, and I've called my dad a couple of times since the wedding. That's it. I don't really even talk to my brother, Dean, but that's because we have a very complicated relationship.

"So, where are you heading?" she asks, adjusting her square-framed glasses higher onto her nose.

"I was actually heading over to the café next door to get something to eat," I tell her, hoping she'll get the hint that I'm starving and just let me go without further small talk. "I'm a little hungover and craving some greasy food."

"Me, too," she agrees. Then her eyes light up. "I'll join you. Elijah is practicing right now, and I'm *so* bored. Seriously, sometimes I regret agreeing to come on this tour."

I try to keep a frown off my face.

While she seems nice and everything, although a little overly cheerful for me, I was planning on just doing whatever I felt like today. If I'm with someone, then everything I do is going to have to be okay with them, too.

Unfortunately, I can't come up with an excuse quickly enough before she loops her arm with mine and practically drags me toward the door.

I grimace. *Well, I guess we're going to lunch together.*

"So, how long have you been married to Micha?" she asks as we start—well, I start walking and she skips—across the parking lot with our arms looped, like we're BFFs or something. But I already have a BFF. Well, two. Micha, who would be holding my hand right now, and Lila, who would never loop arms with me and try to make me skip.

"Um ... for a couple of months," I tell her, swinging to the right to avoid running into a sign.

"Really?" she questions. "Last night, it seemed like maybe you've been married for longer."

"Well, we've known each other for almost our whole lives."

"Aw, that makes sense." She wavers, glancing at me as we reach the doors to the café. "Do you ever worry if stuff will, like, fizzle out? I mean, I've been dating Elijah for only six months and, honestly, sometimes I get kind of bored. I keep suggesting we have a threesome to spice things up, but he hasn't agreed yet. Not that he hasn't disagreed, either."

I wait for her to toss me a joking smile.

She doesn't.

Instead, she opens the café door and the wonderful smell of burgers graces my nostrils.

God, that smells so good.

"Have you ever had one?" she asks as she pulls me into the café with her.

"Have I ever what?" I'm too distracted by the delicious aroma to focus on her completely.

She smiles amusedly at me. "Had a threesome. Like with you and Micha and someone else. Or maybe with someone else you've dated."

My gaze skims around the occupied booths filling up the diner, noting a few people have glanced in our direction. So has the waitress at the register. She may not be speaking extremely loudly, but she's not being very quiet, either.

"Um ... no," I whisper.

She snorts a laugh. "Why are you whispering? It's not that big of a deal."

She approaches the register. "We'd like a booth, please."

The waitress gives her an annoyed look while collecting a couple of menus, and I seize the opportunity to slip my arm from Crazy Pants—and yes, I remember her name, but this one seems more fitting. Then I start plotting my escape.

"Right this way," the waitress says, leading us to a corner booth that is tucked away from most of the customers, a move that I don't think is coincidental.

"Well, she seemed like a total bitch," Remi states before the waitress is out of earshot. Then she collects one of the menus that the waitress practically threw onto the table.

I keep my lips zipped as I pick up the other menu and pretend to look it over. Really, I'm figuring out an excuse to tell her so that I can leave.

"So, I was thinking that maybe you'd be interested," she says casually as she scans over the menu.

"In what?" I ask, hoping she doesn't mean what I thinks she does.

She glances up at me. "In having a threesome with me and Elijah."

She has got to be kidding me. Not that I think it's completely wrong to have a threesome—to each their own—but I'm married and she barely knows me.

I shake my head. "Yeah, I don't think so."

She juts out her lip. "Why not? You're totally

Elijah's type. Not really mine, but I think he'll only agree to it if I find someone who interests his tastes."

I can't … I have no words.

"Um … I need to go to the bathroom." I get up and rush toward the bathrooms.

When I get to the door, though, I steer right and push through the kitchen doors.

"Hey, you can't be in here," the waitress who seated us says.

"I know, but …" I step forward. "Can I just exit through the back door?"

She eyes me over and recognition clicks. "You came in with that girl, right? The one who called me a bitch?"

I nod. "Yep."

"All right. Go ahead." She points toward a door.

I offer her a grateful look then hurry off, glad to be leaving that girl behind, but annoyed because I'm still really hungry.

ELLA

I END up grabbing a bite to eat from a taco place across the street. It's nowhere near as satisfying as a burger would've been, but it gets the job done. After that, I spend the next few hours wandering around the area, going into shops and observing the scenery, which is a lot different from the snowy mountains of Star Grove. I keep expecting Micha to text me, but he never does, something I find a bit odd. That is … until I check my pocket for my phone and realize it's not there.

"Shit," I curse. "Where the crap did it fall out?"

Since I haven't checked my messages for a while, it could be practically anywhere. Still, I attempt to back-track my steps all the way to the café.

I'm a little apprehensive to go in there, and not

because I think Remi will be there waiting for me, but because I'm worried the waitress will remember me. Not that I have anything to be embarrassed about. Remi was the one who called her a bitch. Still, I'm a bit uneasy as I wander inside and see that the same waitress is still working the register.

When she notices me approaching, she gives me a wary smile.

"You're back," she states as she tucks a pen behind her ear.

"Yeah, I can't find my phone," I tell her, resting my arms on the counter. "You haven't found one, have you?"

She shakes her head. "No. I can check in the back, though, if you want me to and see if any of the other waitresses have seen it."

"Yeah, if you could, that'd be great."

She nods and walks off, pushing through a set of double doors.

I sit down in a barstool near the front counter while I wait, hoping Micha hasn't tried to message me. If he has, he's probably worried.

I thrum my fingers against the counter as I grow frustrated, but not with the waitress—I know it's not her fault. I'm more frustrated with myself.

Why didn't I notice my phone was gone earlier?

Because I was too distracted by Crazy Pants.

No more socializing for me. Not that I chose to do it.

"Sorry, hon." The waitress returns to the register. "Unfortunately, no one's seen your phone."

"All right. Well, thanks for checking." I stand up to leave, figuring I'll go back to the hotel room to see if Micha's there by chance.

"One of the waitresses did tell me something that I feel like I should tell you," the waitress says before I walk off.

I twist back around, and she motions for me to come back to the counter. When I do so, she leans in and lowers her voice. "That girl that you were with earlier, she came in here last night with a camera. She sat at one of the tables that has a view of the hotel next door and started taking photos and uploading them to a laptop. Now, I'm not about to pretend that I know anything about photography, but from what I was told, the photos were of some of the room's windows."

"The girl that I came in here with today was here last night?" I question. When the waitress nods, I ask, "About what time?"

"Around midnight or so, I think. I can double-check if you want me to."

"No, it's fine. Thanks for the info." I give her a distracted wave as I push out the exit door and step outside, confusion spinning inside me.

It doesn't make any sense. Last night, around midnight, is when I met Remi. Unless I was too drunk and getting the time wrong. That could be a possibility, but that still doesn't explain why she was sitting in the café, taking photos of the hotel. I mean, I get that photography can be a form of art and maybe she saw something that captured her attention.

I glance up at the building in front of, scanning the windows and getting a good view of the inside of the rooms, at least the ones that have the curtains open.

"So weird," I mumble as I start across the parking lot toward the hotel entrance. However, at the last second, I veer right and decide to take the side entrance to avoid risking crossing paths with that Remi girl.

While she may just be a bit weird, I'd rather not take my chances.

MICHA

I'M TRYING NOT to panic as I pace the hotel room floor, but Ella hasn't been replying to any of my messages. And when I call her, it goes straight to voicemail. I would think that maybe she's off somewhere drawing and has lost track of time, but the sun is setting and it's getting dark outside.

"Come on, baby," I mutter as I try to call her again. And again, it goes straight to voicemail.

Since I've left her at least seven or eight messages already, I hang up and grab my jacket so I can head out to look for her. When we get back, I'm totally going to get us one of those track-your-phone apps.

Hurrying across the room, I grab the door handle and throw the door open, only to find Ella standing on the other side.

"Holy shit," I say, slipping my fingers through hers and pulling her into the room. "Where the heck have you been? I've been trying to call you …" I trail off, telling myself to calm the fuck down. But I didn't even realize how worried I was until now.

I skim over her—her long legs, her lean body, her full lips, big green eyes, and flowing auburn hair. She appears to be okay, but I need to be positive.

"You're okay, right?"

She bobs her head up and down. "Yeah, sorry. I lost my phone and spent about an hour looking for it."

Relief trickles through me. "Did you find it?"

She shakes her head, grimacing. "No. I honestly don't have a clue where I could've lost it, either. I know I had it when I left the room, but that's the last time I saw it. And I walked to a lot of places, so …" She shrugs, seemingly exhausted. "I might need to get a new one."

"We'll do that first thing tomorrow," I assure her, bringing her hand to my lips and placing a soft kiss against her skin. Then I breathe in her scent—strawberries and vanilla. God, I love her scent.

"I'm sorry I worried you," she tells me. "Although, I'm a little surprised you got that worried. It's not like I've never wandered off alone before and not answered my phone."

I kiss her hand one more time before lowering it

from my lips. Then I mold my palm against her cheek. "Pretty girl, we're in a big-ass city that neither of us know our way around, it's dark, you weren't answering your phone, and you hadn't texted me all day. I wasn't worried. I was freaking the fuck out!"

"I'm sorry," she says again. Then she nibbles on her bottom lip as she loops her arms around the back of my neck. "Tell me what to do to make you feel better."

God, I love it when she gets like this. It turns me on so badly that my cock actually hurts.

"While I'd love to fuck you so fucking hard right now," I say, cupping her ass, "I have to perform in, like, an hour."

He cheeks flush at my remark. It's something else I love—how we've been together for so long yet she still gets flushed when I talk dirty to her. I hope that never changes.

"After, though, I'm going to bring you back here, strip your clothes off, and make you moan," I whisper, brushing my lips across hers and making her shiver. Then I pull back, tucking a strand of hair behind her ear. "You're going to watch me perform tonight, right?"

She nods, staring up at me with her big green eyes that are so damn gorgeous. "Yeah." Then she quietly sighs, confusing the hell out of me.

"Do you not want to?" I question, wondering if

maybe she's starting to grow tired of this whole touring thing.

She shakes her head. "No, I want to. It's just that …" She blows out an exasperated sigh as she steps back from me and flops down on the bed, draping her arm over her face. "I just don't want to see that Remi girl again."

"Remi?" I step toward her, nudging her legs open so I can step between them. Then I lean over her, resting my arms beside her head. "Who the heck is that?"

She peers at me from underneath her arm. "The girl we hung out with for a little bit last night. She's dating Elijah. Or, well, I think that's what his name is. Honestly, I can barely remember a lot of last night."

"Yeah, you were kind of drunk." I lean closer to her. "And I know this because you were super horny."

Biting her lip, she shakes her head. "No, I wasn't."

I roll my eyes. "Yeah, you were. You tend to get like that every time you're drunk."

"Liar," she accuses, but she's struggling not to smile.

"Denier," I retort back, lowering my lips toward hers. "Every time you get tipsy, you beg me to touch you, put my face between your legs, fuck you."

"I do not—"

I nip at her lips before she can finish. Then I slip

my tongue into her mouth, and she parts her lips willingly while slipping her hands to my back as she pulls me closer, hitching her legs around my waist. But, while I'd love to stay like this, let her do whatever she wants with me, I have to get going.

I groan, pulling back and breathing heavily. "As much as I want to stay here and let this continue, I have to go or I'm going to be late."

She juts out her bottom lip. "Oh, fine."

I nip at her lip one final time before standing up. "So, are you really not going?"

"No, I'm going." She pushes up onto her elbows. "I just want to avoid Remi."

I head for my suitcase to grab a fresh shirt, since the one I'm currently wearing smells like barbeque sauce, thanks to Mike taking me out to a steakhouse for lunch so we could discuss my career.

He wants me to start working on an album once the tour is over. While I'm excited about the idea, I'm also really fucking nervous. Not just over the idea of creating my own album but because it's going to be a lot of work and a lot of time away from Ella. And I already feel like I barely see her now.

She's been so good about it, too, something I love her more for.

"Why do you want to avoid her?" I ask as I tug off my shirt.

Her gaze skims across my chest before she fixes her gaze on mine. "Because she seems a little ..." She wavers. "I don't even know."

I tug the clean shirt over my head then reach for my leather band that's on the dresser. "Wanna elaborate?"

She shrugs. "This afternoon, when I was heading out to lunch, I ran into her in the lobby. Honestly, I didn't even recognize her, but she acted like we were friends."

"And that's a bad thing?"

"Well, it wouldn't have been totally bad, except she invited herself to lunch with me then asked me if I'd consider having a threesome with her and her boyfriend and loud enough that people in the café heard. And then she called the waitress a bitch, who totally heard her say it."

"She's the one who sounds like a bitch," I say as I fasten the leather band on my wrist. "Doesn't she know you're married?"

She nods. "One of the first things she asked me was if I was your wife."

If Remi hadn't known Ella was married to me, I may have joked off the situation, but the fact that she did makes me wary about the entire thing, especially the threesome proposal. I also have to wonder if Elijah was part of the proposal. I don't know the guy very well, but I'm definitely going to get to the bottom of that. And if he was part of it ... well, we're gonna have a problem.

"There's more," Ella says, sitting up and tucking a strand of her hair behind her ear. "So, after she made the proposal, I said I had to go to the bathroom, but then I snuck out the back door of the café and ditched her. Then I spent the day wandering around the city. After I realized I'd left my phone somewhere, I had to backtrack my steps, which meant I had to go back to the café. And while I was there, the waitress that Remi called a bitch told me that Remi was in the café last night, taking photos of the windows of the hotel room and uploading them onto her computer. Which not only is completely weird, but doesn't seem plausible since Remi was at the bar with us last night. Unless the waitress got the time wrong ... or I was confused about the time we were hanging out at the bar, which could be a possibility. I don't know." She sighs. "The whole situation seems sketchy."

"Yeah, it does," I agree, worry creeping through me.

While I've heard from other bands that stalkers can become a real problem, I don't think I'm popular enough yet to have that issue. But what Ella's telling me has me concerned.

"How about you ride over with me tonight?" I

suggest. "And I can talk to Elijah; see what he knows about all this."

She shakes her head. "I don't want you to have to start drama with someone."

"I won't have to start any drama," I assure her as I walk over and place a kiss on her lips. "Just as long as he understands that you're my wife and that there won't be any more proposals."

She sighs against my lips. "You really don't have to do that. I can deal with Crazy Pants for a few more weeks. Then the tour will be over."

"I don't want you to have to deal with anything." I lean back and cup her cheek. "You're here, supporting me. You changed your life for me. And you deserve to be as comfortable as possible." I don't wait for her to answer, slipping my fingers through hers and pulling her to her feet. "I also wanna take you out after the concert. Just you and me. And then, tomorrow, we'll get you a new phone, because there's no way in hell I'm gonna be comfortable with us not being able to get ahold of each other whenever we need to."

She nods. "Now that, I can agree with you on."

ELLA

THE CONCERT VENUE is at a fairground that's surrounded by desert, the city glittering in the distance. Food trucks have been crammed into the space, and lights are everywhere, lighting up the darkness and reflecting against the night sky. The scene has me wishing I'd brought my sketchbook, but I was too distracted when we left the hotel room.

While I'm grateful Micha wants to make things comfortable for me, I don't want to be responsible for causing drama for him. Go figure. I used to do that shit all the time, but I want to be better for him.

"Are you sure you want to talk to him?" I ask Micha as he scans the backstage area for Elijah.

He looks good tonight in a black shirt, dark jeans, and thick boots. A leather band ornaments his wrist, and his lip ring glints in the lights shining down on us.

He nods, sweeping his fingers through his chin-length, blond hair. "Yeah, it needs to be taken care of."

I resist a frown, leaning against the wall behind me with my arms crossed.

When he glances at me, he smiles amusedly. "Aw, don't pout, pretty girl. I already promised I wouldn't cause any drama."

"No, what you basically said was that you wouldn't cause any drama just as long as Elijah was cooperative."

"Maybe he will be."

"Yeah, maybe." But the fact that he's dating Crazy Pants makes me doubtful.

"There he is," Micha murmurs then starts toward the other side of the stage.

I straighten and follow after him, my gaze roving across the faces until I spot the guy who I think is Elijah.

He's talking to a girl with long, blonde hair, fiery red lips, and she has a nose piercing. She's also sporting a flowery black dress, a leather jacket, and boots. At first glance, I think she's Remi, but when we get closer, I realize she's not. She just looks similar. And familiar.

Where the fuck do I know her from? I think to myself as I slow to a stop beside Micha.

"Hey, how's it going?" Micha greets Elijah with a chin nod, casually reaching over and threading his fingers through mine.

"Good." Elijah, a taller guy with short dark hair and wearing all black, gives Micha a chin nod. "Are you ready for this crowd tonight? I heard this area can bring in a wilder group."

"Yeah, I heard that, too," Micha says, grazing his finger along the inside of my wrist. "Wild can be fun, though."

"Yeah, for sure," Elijah agrees, stuffing his hands into his pockets. "I just wish I wasn't so hungover from last night. Although, I'm blaming that on your wife and Remi." He smiles at me while playfully nudging the girl standing next to him. "Fucking peer pressure, man."

The girl standing next to him smiles and shakes her head. "You didn't have to keep up with us." She kisses his cheek. "You could've said no."

He cocks a brow at her. "And make myself look like a pussy?"

"There's no shame in losing a shot contest to two women," she teases, playfully nudging him in the shoulder. "Which FYI, you still lost despite your efforts." She grins at me. "Ella's pretty badass, though.

Seriously, *I'm* a badass when it comes to taking vodka shots, and she made me look weak."

A memory of last night suddenly bitch smacks me out of nowhere.

Holy freakin' hell. This girl *is* Remi. And the girl from earlier today was not.

Micha's lips part, to say who knows what, but before he gets a chance to speak and maybe start that drama I didn't want him to start, I tug on his arm.

"Hey, can I talk to you for a second?" I give him a pressing look. "It's super important."

His brows knit as he nods. "Sure."

Forcing a smile, I start to tow him toward the other side of the stage.

The girl with Elijah—Remi—calls out, "Hey, Ella, I'm going down to the food trucks later. You wanna hang out?"

"Yeah, sure." I throw her a wave then powerwalk across the stage, not stopping until I reach a secluded area near the back.

"All right, pretty girl, what the hell was that about?" Micha wiggles his hand from mine and crosses his arms, looking at me accusingly. "Is this your way of trying to force me not to confront Elijah?"

I shake my head. "No. This is my way of stopping you from making a mistake."

He sighs heavily. "Baby, this needs to be taken care of—"

I place my finger over his lips, shushing him. "No, it doesn't. Because that girl with Elijah is Remi."

"Okay …" His lips move against my finger. "So, what? You don't want me to confront him in front of her?"

"No, I don't want you to confront him at all, because that girl isn't who I met this morning." I lower my finger from his lips.

His mouth curves into a frown. "What do you mean she wasn't the girl from this morning? I thought you said she was Remi."

"No, she *said* she was Remi. I honestly couldn't really remember her enough to know for sure. Well, until I saw her." I nod my head in the direction of where Elijah and Remi are standing. "Once they started talking about last night, memories started surfacing and I realized the girl from this morning wasn't the girl I did shots with last night. She just pretended to be."

Micha's lips form an *O*, and his eyes widen. "Holy fuck."

"Yeah, holy fuck." I shake my head, a chill breaking across my skin. "And this girl from this morning, she must've known a lot about me, because she somehow knew I wouldn't totally recognize Remi. I should've, though. I mean, she had shorter hair and was wearing glasses, but she said she had contacts and extensions in last night." I swallow hard. "Which means she knows a lot about what I've been doing, that I was hanging out at the bar with Remi the night before, that I was drunk. She also knew Remi was dating Elijah."

Micha shakes his head as he absorbs all this. "Why the hell would someone do that? I mean, what's the point?"

"I have no idea," I say. "But it's creepy, especially since the waitress said she was in the diner last night, taking photos of the hotel room windows."

Wariness floods Micha's expression. "I hate to tell you this, but I'm pretty sure the curtains weren't closed last night when I fucked you."

My eyes widen. "*What?*"

He offers me an apologetic look. "Sorry, but you basically almost took off your clothes in the elevator and tried to suck my dick. It took all my willpower just to get you into the room with your clothes on and my pants zipped up. The moment we got into the room, I stopped fighting you and let you do whatever you wanted, which was a lot of dirty, very distracting things. So, closing the curtains was the last thing on my mind."

Normally, when he talks about stuff like this, he's

all teasing smiles and playful winks. But he looks very serious right now, revealing he's worried.

"What should we do?" I ask. "I mean, do we just let it go?"

He nibbles on his lip ring. "I don't know. I guess that all depends on if this weirdo poser tries to contact us again." He rubs his jawline, his gaze wandering back over to the other side of the stage. "Maybe I should talk to Elijah about it. If this woman knew stuff about him and Remi, maybe they know who she is."

"Yeah, that's a good idea."

He takes my hand, brushes his lips across my knuckles, and then pulls me with him as he makes his way over to where Elijah and Remi are standing, talking and laughing about something.

"You're back." Remi smiles as we approach them.

"Yeah, we actually kind of have a weird question to ask you," Micha tells her. "It's about a girl that approached Ella this morning, pretending to be you."

Remi's forehead creases. "What?"

Micha nods. "Yeah, it was really strange."

Then he and I give them a quick rundown of what happened. By the time we're finished, they both appear worried.

"I don't want to scare you"—Remi glances from

Micha to me—"but you might have a stalker on your hands."

"It happens sometimes," Elijah adds, slipping his arm behind Remi and pulling her closer, "when a fan gets too obsessed. Unfortunately, the laws on stalking are very vague."

"Which is his way of saying there basically really aren't any laws against stalking," Remi states with a frown. "At least, not any that come with real consequences."

"You sound like you're speaking from experience," I say, leaning into Micha as goosebumps sprout across my flesh. I'm not cold, though. In fact the air is warm and dry. I'm just unsettled.

"I am," Remi tells me. "A couple of months ago, there was this woman who wouldn't leave Elijah alone. She went to every one of his concerts, got backstage passes, and followed him around. Which, whatever. I get the whole fan thing. But then she started showing up at the hotels we were staying at, the restaurant we dined in—she was everywhere."

"Jesus," Micha breathes out. "What'd you guys end up doing?"

Remi lifts a shoulder. "Nothing. We filed reports with the police several times, but since she never technically did anything that was considered breaking the law, it didn't matter." Remi nods at the field area, crammed with fans waiting for the show to start. "She's probably down there right now."

My wide eyes skate to the crowd as I press closer to Micha. Is this really happening? Does Micha actually have a stalker?

"But, wouldn't I have to be a bit more popular before I have to worry about shit like that?" Micha asks, tucking my head underneath his chin.

"No. I had my first issue with a stalker back when I was in high school and still playing at talent shows and shit," Elijah says. "Granted, it was easier to deal with back then. Still … popularity doesn't mean anything when it comes to this. And, while I don't want to scare the shit out of you, I feel like I should probably stress that the more popular you get, the more shit like what happened with that girl today will happen."

"But, what was even the point?" I straighten, looking at Elijah. "I mean, why try to have lunch with me? What does that do for her?"

"You said she tried to convince you to have a threesome, right?" Remi asks, and I nod. "Well, my bet is that was her way of trying to get you to cheat on Micha, so she could break you up. Stella—the girl who stalks Elijah—does shit like that all the time. Also, if I were you, I'd make sure to start closing your curtains in your room. And I'd cancel your phone ASAP, because my bet is she jacked it."

I can't … There are no words.

"I'm sorry to pile all this shit on you," Remi says. "I just feel like you should know what to expect so you can avoid situations like what happened today."

I nod, uneasiness flowing through me. "No, I appreciate it. I'm just … It's a lot to take in."

"It is," Remi agrees. "I can give you some pointers on the best way to deal with it. When the concert starts, we can grab something to eat and go find somewhere to sit down and talk."

"Yeah, that sounds nice … Thanks," I say distractedly, and she gives me a sympathetic look.

"I'm gonna go grab my guitar and start getting ready," Micha announces as his phone buzzes from inside his pocket. Then he looks at me. "You wanna go with me then meet Remi around back in just a few?"

"Sure." I look at Remi. "Is that cool with you?"

She nods. "See you in ten?"

"That works," I tell her.

"Awesome." She throws me a wave as Micha steers me away toward the area where his guitar is kept.

The space back there is buzzing with energy, musicians rushing around, getting ready to perform.

Instead of stopping in the middle of it, Micha

guides me to the far back corner where it's way less noisier.

"I'm so fucking sorry." He cups my face between his hands. "I hate that I just put this tremendous amount of stress on you."

"You didn't do it. Crazy Pants did."

"But she's only doing this because of me."

"So? You can't help it if you're sexy, charming, and an amazing singer," I compliment the crap out of him in an attempt to lighten the mood, but he continues to frown. I sigh. "Micha, you can't blame yourself for this. This girl … she obviously has problems, and that in no way is your fault."

"I know, but …" A sigh eases from his lips. "I brought you into this … If I would've realized something like this would happen, I wouldn't have talked you into going with me … I just … I love having you with me, and honestly, I didn't think anything like this would happen."

"Stop worrying," I press. "Technically, nothing really has happened, except for some girl trying to convince me to have a threesome and cheat on you, which I never, ever would."

"She also probably took photos of us," Micha stresses. "And jacked your phone. That's crossing a line."

He's right, but I don't want him to worry. Not when he's about to perform.

"I'll turn off my phone right now." I stick out my hand. "Just give me your phone, and I'll call the phone company. That'll be one less problem we need to solve."

Still frowning, he sticks his hand into his pocket and digs out his phone. "Your phone's password protected, right?"

I nod as he unlocks his phone. "Of course."

"Good. The last thing I want is for this creeper to see all those dirty texts we send each other."

"Agreed." I reach to take his phone, but he clutches it, paling.

"Are you sure your phone's password protected?" he asks, glancing up at me.

I nod. "I put a four digit passcode on it."

Nervousness edges across his features. "Well, I think this creeper cracked it."

"What?" I exclaim. "Why would you think that?"

"Because I just received this text." He shows me the screen of his phone.

The Most Important Person in the World to Me: Hey, baby, wanna meet up with me later? I've got a big surprise for you.

If I weren't so upset, his name for me would've

made me smile, but the situation is way too creepy for me to smile.

"So, is she pretending to be me?" I question. "Or does she just think this'll lure you to her?"

He glances at the phone again, his frown deepening. "I think the latter."

"Why's that?" I ask, but then he shows me the screen again and I have my answer.

Crazy Pants has just sent him a photo of her naked.

"Yeah, let me get my phone turned off now." I take the phone from him, look up the phone company's number, and call.

Five minutes later, my phone is turned off but messages from Crazy Pants were buzzing through up until the very last second of the disconnection.

Jesus, this is intense. And stressful. I've never been one for handling stress very well, but I'm going to have to learn how to do this.

I need to be strong.

Need to keep my shit together.

For Micha.

Speaking of which, Mike pulled Micha aside while I was on the phone to chat about something. I can't see them anywhere, and Micha is about to go on stage soon. I deliberate whether or not to track him down now or wait until after the performance. I'm just about to decide the latter when Micha returns.

"Did you get your phone turned off?" he asks, adjusting the guitar he has strapped around him.

I nod, moving to hand him his phone. "When I get a new phone, they said to call and they'll change over the service, or I can just have them do it at the store."

Shaking his head, he pushes my hand back toward me. "You hold on to that. I don't want you wandering around without a phone on you."

"But the only person I call is you, pretty much."

"Still … Just in case."

"Just in case of what?"

He shrugs and kisses my cheek. "I have to go on in just a few minutes. Be safe and don't wander off alone."

"I won't," I promise. "Now stop worrying about me and focus on kicking ass out there."

He forces a smile onto his face, letting me know that's probably the last thing that'll ever happen.

I internally sigh. Micha always puts me first before everything, and until he knows I'm safe, he'll stress himself out.

I need to find a way to fix this stalker problem.

Somehow.

ELLA

I WATCH Micha sing from the side of the stage area for a while before meeting up with Remi to chitchat about this stalker. She wants to grab something to eat, and while I am hungry, I also want to watch Micha, so I suggest just chatting backstage, but she insists that she's starving.

"Don't worry; you'll still be able to see him from the food trucks," she tells me when I hesitate.

I guess she makes a good point.

"Okay," I agree.

I follow her down the stairway that leads to the field where food trucks are scattered about, the area crammed with people.

"So, how long have you and Micha been together?" she shouts over the noise surrounding the stage.

"Well, we've been married for only a couple of months and have been dating on and off for a couple of years," I tell her "But we've been best friends since we were kids and we were pretty much inseparable, except for on a few occasions." Those occasions being when I had to work on trying to heal myself, but I'm not about to say that aloud.

"That explains a lot," she muses, her eyes sparkling in the reflection of the lights glittering across the darkness from the stage.

I swing around a couple of people talking and smoking. "What do you mean?"

She shrugs, tucking her hands into the pockets of her jacket. "I just mean you two seem really connected in a way a lot of people aren't. I mean, don't get me wrong; I'm totally connected with Elijah, but I've only known him for like six months and there's still a lot for me to learn about him." Her boots scuff the dirt as she sidesteps around a beer bottle. "Honestly, I wasn't going to even come on this tour, but one thing lead to another and …" She shrugs, her eyes seeming haunted by something.

I can't quite place what, but knowing I've had a similar look in my eyes, I don't ask. I'm not one for prying into other people's personal business.

"It's good I came, though," she mutters more to herself, dazing off for a moment, but then she blinks back to reality, putting a smile on her face as we stop near the food truck.

"So, what're you thinking? Tacos? Burgers? I think there might even be a pizza place at one of these?"

Remembering how much I wanted a burger earlier, I say, "Let's go with burgers."

"Awesome. Sounds good to me." She smiles as she starts toward a truck that has burger everything on the menu.

Remi seems like a happy person to me, her smile bright and shiny. It makes me question how well we're going to get along, seeing as how I'm not the most cheerful person in the world. But I'm going to try my best to be upbeat. Plus, Lila and I are kind of opposites and we get along.

After we order and get out food, we head toward the back of the crowd where we have a good view of the stage but don't have to be surrounded by sweaty people.

I watch Micha on stage as I take a bite of my burger. He's strumming his guitar as he pours his soul into the microphone, the lights shining down on him. Even though I've seen him sing on stage a ton of times, I still find him sexy. So, so sexy.

"So, about this whole stalker situation," Remi starts as she unwraps her burger, drawing my attention to her. "I was trying to think of a few good pointers for you, something that'd make you feel more at ease with this entire situation, but then I decided that being honest is probably better." She takes a bite of her burger. "That is, if you're cool with that. I mean, honesty is probably a bit scarier in this situation, but at the same time, sugarcoating shit isn't going to do you any good when reality sets in."

"Okay." Wariness creeps inside me as I chew another bite of burger.

"Okay." She gives a considering pause. "The truth about all this is that dealing with this sort of shit—stalkers, obsessive fans shit—is going to be a pain in the ass. I've heard horror stories from people about fans going too far. And like Elijah said, the laws on stalking are super lax, so unless your stalker completely and totally crosses the line into illegal, the cops won't do shit."

I frown. "So, what? I'm supposed to just let this crazy woman invade my and Micha's lives?"

She shakes her head. "No. You can totally fight back, but you need to be careful with how much and what kind of attention you give her, because it might just feed more into her delusional world. And I'd try to keep Micha from getting involved as much as possible, because that's probably what she wants—his attention. If that makes any sense."

"I guess it does." I move to take another bite of my burger, but I'm not feeling very hungry anymore.

"I'm sorry," she tells me. "I wish I could tell you something better."

"It's fine. It's not your fault," I assure her. "I just wish there was an easier way to handle this other than trying to pretend it doesn't exist."

"Well, you don't have to pretend it doesn't exist. And you do need to be careful. Ignoring her completely might lead to a disastrous outcome."

She doesn't specify what that means, but she doesn't really have to. It's enough to make me extremely worried about what's to come.

ELLA

AFTER REMI'S OMINOUS WARNING, our conversation sort of fizzles. I mean, we make small chitchat and everything, but my head is stuck in the *what ifs*, even after Micha's performance is over and we navigate back toward the stage area to meet up with Micha and Elijah.

What if this stalker is straight up insane? She already seems like it to me.

And then, to make matters worse, thoughts of the girl being insane shift to my own mental issues and my mom's.

Over the years, my mom slowly lost touch with reality to the point where some strange things occurred, mysterious things that I still don't have the answers to. Like the one time she was suspected of foul play against a neighbor of ours, though nothing ever came of it. And I'm sure she wasn't really involved ...

I think, anyway.

"Hey." A soft breath tickles my ear as arms envelop me.

I startle, only for the voice to register a split-second later. "Hey." I grab Micha's arms and pull him closer.

Remi has already wandered off to go find Elijah, but she told me she'll catch up with me later.

"Is everything okay?" he whispers worriedly in my ear.

He knows me so well that sometimes it's frightening.

I nod. "Yeah, I was just thinking about some stuff."

"About this whole stalker thing?" he asks. "Because I don't want you to worry about it. I'll take care of it. Nothing will ever happen to you."

I shake my head, twisting around to face him. "I don't want you to worry about that, either. Or take care of it." I loop my arms around the back of his neck. "Remi said it's probably better if we don't give this stalker too much attention, anyway. That it'll only feed more into what she's doing."

He sucks on his lip ring, studying me. "I get that—I

really do—but I'm not just going to ignore the fact that this woman is causing stress for you."

"I'm not stressed," I insist.

He gives me a *really* look. "Pretty girl, I've been glancing over here for the last fifteen minutes, and every time, you were dazed off."

"I wasn't dazing off about that," I tell him. When he gives me a dubious look, I add, "I promise I wasn't. I was actually thinking about the past."

His brows knit. "What sort of stuff about the past?"

I lift a shoulder. "That one time my mom was a suspect for that whole neighbor thing."

Recognition clicks. "Oh yeah, I remember that." His brows furrow. "Why were you thinking about that?"

I shrug. "I don't know. It just popped into my head." I don't want to tell him that I was thinking about my and my family's mental health issues, mostly because he'll probably stress out that I'm going to that dark place again, which I'm not.

"Because you're stressed," he states the obvious.

"I am," I admit then yawn. "I'm also really tired."

He wets his lips with his tongue then traces the pad of his finger back and forth along my bottom lip. "Let's get you back to the hotel room then."

"You don't need to do anything else?"

"Nah. I mean, there's a little get-together that one of the bands is having, but I can blow it off."

My lips curve downward. "You don't have to blow stuff off just because I'm tired. You should go. I can go back to the hotel by myself and go to sleep."

He rolls his eyes. "Yeah, that's not going to fucking happen."

"Micha …" I start, not wanting him to miss out on stuff because I'm exhausted.

He places a finger against my lips, shushing me. "I'd always rather be with you. You are at the top of my want list, pretty girl, whether you like it or not."

My lips turn upward. I can't help smiling when he says stuff like that to me.

"You're at the top of my want list, too," I tell him.

His eyes glitter under the backstage lights. "Yeah?"

My heart flutters in my chest. "Yeah."

Now his eyes blaze with that want he just told me about. "Let's get you back to the hotel room then."

I nod, knowing I won't be going to sleep as soon as we get back to the hotel room. And even though I'm tired and hungover, I'm completely okay with that.

ELLA

By the time Micha and I make it back to the hotel room, thoughts of the stalker and the past are no longer plaguing my mind. All I can think about is him —how safe I feel with him and how amazing he smells.

"Did you eat anything yet?" he asks as we enter the room. Then he closes the door behind us and locks it.

I nod, sitting down on the bed and taking off my shoes. "Yeah, I ate a burger with Remi while I watched you perform."

"Okay. Well, I'm starving, so I'm going to order room service." He crosses the room, peers out the window, and then closes the curtain.

And that's when all the crap that happened today returns.

"You want anything?" he asks as he picks up a menu from off the nightstand and sits down on the edge of the bed.

"Hmmm ..." I crawl across the bed and over to him. "What do they have for dessert?"

"Let's see." He turns the page with one hand while absentmindedly playing with my hair with the other. "They have cheesecake."

"That sounds good." I lean into his touch, seeking comfort in it.

He tilts his head and presses an unexpected kiss to my lips. "Let me call this in, and then I'm going to kiss the hell out of you, okay?"

I nod, brushing my lips across his. Then I scoot back toward the headboard and wait for him as he calls in the order. The entire time, he looks at me, chewing on his bottom lip. Figuring we could both use the distraction, I decide to mess with him, trailing my hands down my body. He stumbles over his words then shakes his head, finishes up, and hangs up the phone.

"You're so asking for it," he teases as he moves over to me and lines his body over mine.

"You say that like it's a bad thing," I tease right back, placing my hands on his back and pushing him closer. Then I hitch my legs around his waist and grind against him.

He groans, closing his eyes and delving his fingers into my hips. "We have to take it slow until room service gets here, or they'll end up interrupting."

"What? You can't make it quick?" I whisper hotly in his ear.

He groans again, his grip on me tightening. "Pretty girl, I want to …" He trails off, shivering as I nip at his earlobe. "Fuck," he breathes out, skating his hands toward the button of my pants. He unfastens it then slips his hands downward, into my panties, and then inside me.

Now I'm the one to moan, lowering my eyelids as I clutch his shoulder blades.

"God, you always feel so good," he murmurs as he places soft kisses across my jawline.

"So do you," I whisper, slipping one of my hands down the front of his jeans and start rubbing him.

He breathes heavily. "God, I fucking love you." He grinds his hips against my hand.

"I love you, too," I whisper as I feel myself drift away.

And I'm about to let myself drift, let go and enjoy the moment, when someone knocks on the door.

Micha and I both let out a frustrated groan.

Then a crinkle forms between Micha's brows. "There's no way that can be room service."

I struggle to catch my breath. "Maybe it's Mike."

"Maybe. But he always calls before he comes over."
He continues to look puzzled as he climbs off me.

I lie back on the bed, my heart racing from the almost orgasm. "Whoever it is, I seriously want to kick their ass for ruining that for me."

He throws me a grin from over his shoulder. "Don't worry; I'll take care of you in just a minute."

I smile, and he winks at me before turning, adjusting himself, and then peering out the peephole.

"What the hell?" he mutters, wrapping his fingers around the door handle.

I push up on my elbows, worry stirring inside me. "What's wrong?"

He shakes his head then glances at me. "There's no one there." Worry fills his aqua eyes, which makes my worry soar through the roof.

I stand up and start to make my way over to him, but he holds up his hand.

"Stay right there."

"Micha, maybe you shouldn't open it …" I trail off as he cracks open the door. Then he cautiously sticks his head out into the hallway before opening the door completely and stepping out. He looks left then right then glances down. Then he crouches down, scoops something up, and hurries inside.

"What is that?" I walk over to him as he shuts the door and locks it.

He turns toward me with a red envelope in his hand. "This was on the floor in front of our door."

I tense. "What's in it?"

He feels the envelope. "It feels like there's just a piece of paper in it."

I chew on my thumbnail. "Maybe you shouldn't open it."

He rubs his lips together as he studies the envelope then looks up at me. "I want to know what's in it."

I kind of do, too, but at the same time, I don't.

"It could just be an invitation to something," he says, but I can tell he doesn't think so.

"I really doubt it is, since it was just dropped in front of the door and it's not even addressed to anyone." I give a short pause. "Maybe it's not even for us."

"Maybe." Again, he doesn't sound like he believes it.

And again, I feel the same way.

He rubs his lips together. "I'm going to open it."

I want to argue with him, but before I can, he tears the envelope open. I hold my breath as he takes out the piece of paper that's inside it and unfolds it. Then his forehead creases with confusion.

I inch toward him. "What is it?"

"It's a website." He looks at me and shows me the front of the paper.

On it is a web address printed in black ink.

"That's all that's on it?" I ask warily.

He turns the paper over then nods. "Yeah."

I rub my hands up and down my arms as goose-bumps sprout across my flesh. "Okay … Why was this in front of our door? And what's the website to?"

He shrugs. "There's only one way to find out." He starts past me and toward the laptop sitting on the desk.

I capture a hold of his arm. "Micha, I have a bad feeling about this."

He offers me a forced smile. "It's going to be okay. I'm sure it's probably just like an advertisement for a business or something."

"Then, why do we have to check at all?" I question.

"I don't know." He gives a stiff shrug.

"I know you're lying to me," I inform him. "You're trying to protect me, because you have a bad feeling about this … Like maybe it has to do with the stalker."

He doesn't disagree with me right away, so I know I'm right.

Sighing, he sets the paper and envelope down on the desk then cups my face between his hands. "I'm going to protect you like I promised, but I can't do that if I'm not sure what I'm protecting you from."

He's right. Neither one of us can protect each other if we don't know what's going on.

"Okay, look it up," I say quietly.

Nodding, he gives me a soft kiss then turns around and opens the laptop. He types the address into the search engine.

"I'm not going to go to the address first," he explains. "I want to see if the search engine pulls up anything about it."

"That's a good idea." I take a seat in the chair that's beside the desk and nervously fidget with the leather band that's on my wrist as I watch him read through the results. After a minute ticks by, I can't take the unknowing any longer. "Did you find anything?"

He sighs. "Not really." He tensely massages the back of his neck. "I'm going to go onto the site." He glances at me. "You've got a good virus software protection program on this, right?"

I nod. "Yeah."

"Okay." He takes a deep breath then types in the web address.

Me? I hold my breath, hoping that it is just some weird advertisement for a business, knowing that's probably not the case. But nothing could've prepared me for what's on the site.

"Shit," Micha says at the same time fear pulsates through me.

Because, not only are there naughty photos of me that were on my phone on that website, but so is a video of last night when Micha and I were having sex. And the most frightening thing of all is that the video was taken *inside* our motel room.

MICHA

I'M PRETTY sure I've never felt so much rage in my life as when I saw what was on that website. And the sight of Ella's horrified face made that rage build. I decided right then and there that we needed to call the cops.

I know Remi and Elijah said there wasn't much the cops would do when it came to stalking, but this —these videos and photos—seems like they go beyond that. Whoever took the video was clearly in our hotel room, which means they had to have broken into it. Well, either that or they have a connection with someone at the hotel.

It takes the police about twenty minutes to show up, and by the time they do, Ella has reached a very silent state. I don't like it. At all. Usually, when she gets this quiet about things, it means she's stuck in her own head. I'm not going to let that happen. I'm going to get this taken care of—get that site shut down and get this stalker out of our lives.

Of course, talking to the police kick my optimism down a notch.

"The problem with these things is that whoever did this didn't technically break any laws," one of the officers says as he stands in the middle of the room with his partner beside him.

Ella is sitting on the bed with her arms folded around herself, and I'm standing in front of the officers, trying not to lose my cool.

"That's total bullshit," I snap. "They broke into the room to take that video."

"Did they, though?" the taller of the officers says. "Or did they get ahold of a video that perhaps you two made and just don't want to admit it?"

"If I made a sex video with my wife, I wouldn't be ashamed of it," I tell him, crossing my arms. "But we haven't made one. I promise you that."

"The photos that were taken were from her phone," the officer points out as his partner jots down a note.

"Yeah, so? That's not a crime," I stress, growing more frustrated by the moment. "And FYI, those photos were from a phone that was stolen."

"That could be possible, but from what we've been

told, the phone also could've just been dropped," the officer replies.

I shake my head, my jaw ticking. "If you're not going to help, then why don't you just get the hell out of here?" Under my breath, I mutter, "Fucking asshole."

These officers remind me so much of the ones back in Star Grove—hardly ever wanting to lift a finger.

I thought it was a small town thing, but I was clearly wrong.

"Look, we're sorry," his partner speaks for the first time in a while. "But unfortunately, these types of cases are complicated to take on. However, we will look into it, and we can try to get the website taken down and see if we can find out who the owner is. Although, that can prove to be difficult since almost anyone can create a website these days." He shifts his weight. "I'd also recommend that you report it, as well. Maybe between the both of us, we can get it down."

Unlike his partner, I can tell he's trying to help us. But I don't just want the website taken down. I want this stalker caught, or I have a feeling things are only going to get worse. And I can't let worse become part of Ella's life. I made a vow to her and myself that I would take care of her. Protect her. Make sure she's safe. And I'll do whatever it takes to make sure that happens.

Even if it means having to talk her into going someplace safe.

Even if it means we have to be a part.

ELLA

THE POLICE OFFER us no sense of comfort, and I can tell Micha is pissed off. By the time they leave, he looks like he wants to punch a wall, something I saw him do once when I lied to him and told him I cheated on him. I never have, but at the time, I thought I was doing it to protect him from getting dragged down by me. The only way I could figure out how was for him to believe that I'd cheated on him. And it worked ... for a while. But then Lila outed me. And, while I was a little upset with her at the time, now I'm super grateful.

I can't imagine what would've happened if she didn't. Maybe Micha and I wouldn't be together now.

That thought makes my chest feel tight.

"Hey, this isn't over yet." Micha crouches down in front of me and meets my gaze.

I'm sitting on the bed and have been staring at the floor for who knows how long. While the police were here, room service showed up with our food, so the air smells like greasy food, which makes my gut churn. I'd been eager for dessert before I saw those photos and the video. Now I feel sick to my stomach.

"We're going to get that website down," Micha continues, cupping my face between his hands.

I nod, but I know it's not going to be that easy, that those photos and the video might be online for a while. And even if they get taken down, Crazy Pants still has them.

"I still can't believe she managed to take a video of us while we were having sex," I mumble as Micha stands up, but only to sit down beside me. "How did we not notice?"

He shakes his head. "I have no idea. I mean, I know we were a little tipsy and the room was kind of dark, but there was a little light flowing from the bathroom. Plus, the video looked like it was taken from where the desk was …" He trails off as we both turn around and look at the desk.

He's right. There really isn't any place where she could've been hiding, except maybe in the curtain. Or …

"Wait a second." I rise to my feet and hurry over to the laptop. My heart thunders in my chest as I open up the webcam application and do a search through the videos.

"Fuck," I whisper when I see it—the video taken from last night.

"What is it?" Micha asks as he leans over my shoulder.

"She wasn't in the room. She hacked into the webcam or the iCloud—I'm not sure which. That's how she did it." I slam the laptop shut, my heart thrashing in my chest as I twist around to face him. "Micha, this isn't just a crazed fan. This is … crazy." I can't think of any other word.

"I know." He swallows hard. "This is all my fault."

My brows rise to my hairline. "Why would you say that?"

He lifts a shoulder. "You're here because of me. And this woman is doing this because of me." He shakes his head, his jaw set tight. "I never should've asked you to just bail out on your life and come on the road with me."

Hurt pierces my chest. "You don't want me here?"

His expression softens. "Baby, you know that's not it. I'm just frustrated with myself for making you come on tour with me. If I hadn't, maybe none of this would be happening."

I place my hands on his shoulders. "First of all, you didn't force me to come on tour with you. I chose to, because I want to be with you. And secondly, I'm sure this woman would still be stalking you. She'd probably just be doing it a different way."

He shakes his head from side to side, wisps of his blond hair falling into his eyes. "I don't know … Maybe you're right. But this is all extremely unsettling. And I know I need to get ahold of the police and tell them about the webcam, but part of me wonders if there's even any point."

"I know," I agree. "They seemed like they couldn't care less about this."

Remi had warned me about this, too, but I didn't think things could get this bad and the cops still not be able to do anything. I mean, what has to happen in order for them to be able to do something?

The ideas that come to mind make me shiver and my gut twists. And that nauseating feeling grows as I think about that damn video.

"Seeing that video made me feel icky," I divulge. "I kind of want to take a shower." Like I can simply wash off what happened, though I know it's not going to be that easy.

He tucks a strand of hair behind my ear. "Go ahead and take one. I'll try to get ahold of the domain for the site and see what I need to do to take it down."

"Are you sure?" I ask. "I can help if you need me."

"I can handle it," he promises, brushing his lips across mine. "Go take a shower and try to relax."

I nod, knowing that's not going to be possible, but not wanting him to know that.

I grab some pajamas before heading to the shower, telling Micha, "We probably shouldn't use my computer until we have it looked at."

"Yeah, you're probably right." He fishes his phone out of his pocket. "I'll use my phone to contact the website, and then we'll take your laptop somewhere tomorrow to have it looked at."

I nod then head into the bathroom to take a shower. It's my second one of the day, but the first one was merely to clean off the grime of last night. This one is an attempt to relax the stiffness that has embedded into my muscles.

This isn't the first time I've tried to take a shower to relax myself from the craziness. I used to do it all the time when I was younger, only those showers would often be cold ones due to either the hot water tank not working or the power being shut off because I couldn't pay the bills, because my dad quit or got fired from another job.

I TAKE A LONGER shower than planned, and by the time I get out, my skin is looking a little bit pruney. I feel a little bit better, though. Or at least cleaner. I know the feeling isn't going to last, especially if stuff like what happened tonight keeps happening. The problem is this stalker hasn't made a point as to what she's trying to do. Or, well, not a clear point.

Maybe if we figure that out, we could find a way to get her to stop, I think to myself as I exit the bathroom.

My hair is damp and hanging down my back, and I only have a T-shirt on, so goosebumps dot my flesh the moment I enter the bedroom where the temperature is a bit lower.

Micha is sitting on the bed when I walk in, staring down at his phone, worry creasing his features.

I hate that he's worried. I want him to be happy. But he's not going to be while this is going on.

"So, how'd contacting the domain go?" I ask as I straddle his lap.

He sets the phone down and settles his hands on my waist. "Honestly, it didn't go. I'm still trying to figure out how to contact them. I think it's a really small domain company. They seem pretty damn wary on listing any contact info on their site."

"Well, that sucks." I kiss him, because he looks like he needs a kiss.

"Yeah, it does," he agrees, combing his fingers

through my damp hair, wariness taking over the worry in his expression. "I'll figure it out. It just might take some time. That being said, something else happened while you were in the shower."

I stiffen. "Please tell me she didn't take another video or something?"

He promptly shakes his head. "No, it's nothing like that. It actually doesn't have anything to do with the crazy stalker bitch."

I relax a smidgeon. "Oh. Then, what does it have to do with?"

"Your dad," he tells me cautiously, knowing me well enough to understand that my dad is a touchy subject. Sure, our relationship isn't as bad as it used to be, but that can't erase the past. Nothing can. That I know all too well. "He called me while you were in the shower."

"What? Why did he call you?" He barely calls me as it is.

"Well, he called my phone because he tried to call you, but yours was disconnected," he tells me.

"Right," I say, suddenly realizing that everyone who tries to call me right now is going to have the same problem. Not that I have a ton of people calling me, but still …

"What did he want?" I wonder, shifting my weight.

When Micha hesitates, I suddenly grow worried that maybe my dad relapsed or something.

"Wait—is he okay?"

Micha nods, cupping my cheek and skimming his thumb along my cheekbone. "I don't want you to freak out." Then he mutters more to himself, "Fuck, why did this have to happen right now? Or at all?"

"Micha, just tell me what it is," I demand as I get more panicky.

His worry-filled eyes meet mine. "It's about that case that your mom was a suspect in," he tells me quietly. "It's been reopened and, apparently, your mom's still a suspect."

ELLA

I'm not sure how to react. I've known there was always a possibility of this happening since the case was never solved. But it was considered a cold case, so I just thought ... Well, I don't know what I thought.

What I do know is that I find it freakishly weird that this happens right when this whole stalker thing does. And when I've been thinking about the case all day.

What a fucking freakish coincidence.

A twisted, freakish coincidence.

Why do I feel like it's not a freakish coincidence?

But, what else could it be?

"So, what does that mean?" I ask. "Well, I know what it means, but why did my dad call to tell me about it?"

"I think partly to give you a heads-up that the police might be contacting you," he says. "I also think he might just be stressed out about it and needed someone to talk to."

I crinkle my nose. "I don't really want to talk about it, though." Don't want to talk about an extremely stressful period of my life that negatively was connected with my mom.

"I know. And you don't have to if you don't want to."

"I don't."

"Then we won't." He leans forward and places a kiss on my lips. "Anything you want, I'll give you." He slants back, takes my hand, and places my palms against his chest where I can feel his heart steadily beating. "This belongs to you, pretty girl. If you hurt, I hurt."

"I don't want you to hurt," I whisper.

No, what I want is for things to go back to how they were yesterday, all stress-free and light. But if there's one thing I've learned from my bumpy past, it's that life always has its ups and downs. And I just have to learn how to deal with them the best I can. Dealing being the keyword.

So, while I don't want to, I know what I have to do.

I let out a heavy sigh. "Give me your phone so I can call my dad."

He gives me a hesitant look. "Are you sure?"

I nod. "If I don't call him, I'm just going to sit here and overanalyzing all the things that could be going on."

He allows a few seconds to tick by, as if waiting for me to retract my decision. When I don't, a quiet sigh eases from his lips, and then he gives me his phone.

I take it, and then hover my finger over the button that dials my dad's number. I'm hesitant, worried that whatever he has to say is going to make me crumble. I hate that I feel this way whenever my dad comes into the picture. I wish things were different. Maybe they will be some day after I've had time to heal from the wounds of my past.

Sucking a deep breath, I push dial then put the phone up to my ear.

"Hello?" my dad answers after three rings.

"Hey, it's me ... Ella," I say, chewing on my thumbnail. "Micha said you called."

"Oh. Yeah. Hey." He sounds scattered, but at least he isn't slurring his words. "I'm glad you called me back ... Did Micha tell you why I called?"

"Yeah, he told me that the case Mom was a suspect in is getting reopened and that she's still a suspect."

It's strange to be talking about my mom with him when, in the past, he used to get upset every time she was mentioned.

"Good. I'm glad he told you." He sinks into silence, leaving me confused.

What does he want?

Micha observes me worriedly then mouths, *"Is everything okay?"*

I nod, even though I'm not certain it is. But I don't want him to worry more than he already is.

"Did you need something else?" I ask my dad, wondering if maybe he didn't want me to return his call.

"Actually, I do," he finally says but with a lot of hesitancy. "I need to go through some of your mom's old stuff that I still have. There's actually something I'm looking for. But …" Another long pause. "I'm kind of nervous about doing it. Going through her belong-ings, I mean. My sponsor's a little bit worried, too."

"You think you'll slip up if you do it?"

"Maybe."

Well, at least he's admitting it. That still doesn't explain what he wants from me.

"I'm glad you admitted that, Dad. I really am," I tell him. "But I'm a little confused about what you want me to do or say."

"I know. And it's probably because I'm nervous

about asking you for this—for anything really." Anxiety rings in his tone.

The fact that he's nervous makes me nervous, too.

Micha must sense this, as he starts tracing his fingers up and down my back in a soothing gesture. I melt into his touch, resting my head on his shoulder.

"Go ahead and ask, Dad." I cross my fingers that I'm not making a mistake, that he's not going to say something mean. He hasn't been like that for a while, but there was a very long time when he was always mean to me. "It's okay."

An uneven breath flows through the phone. "I was wondering if there was any way you could come visit for a little bit and help me go through your mom's stuff. I know you're on the road and everything, so I understand if you can't, but I thought I'd ask."

He wants me to come visit.

Okay, this is so weird.

Even weirder is the idea of going through my mom's things. The last time that happened was when that lawyer sent me an old diary of hers that my grandma had.

Still, perhaps I could handle it. Although …

"I thought the house was getting foreclosed." I slant back, looking at Micha, who has question marks flooding his eyes.

"Oh, no, I actually paid the past due amount," he tells me. "Shit, I must've forgotten to tell you."

While him not telling me isn't that big of a surprise, the fact that he found the money to pay the overdue amount is definitely weird.

"How'd you manage that?" I ask.

"Oh, I just ran into a little bit of extra cash," he replies vaguely.

My dad may be sober now, but back in the day, he did a lot of sketchy things, so I question if he got the money in a sketchy way.

"It wasn't illegally, was it?" I hate to ask, but feel like I need to know, especially if I'm going to go back to Star Grove. The last thing I need is to return and find my dad selling drugs out of the house or something.

While I used to not mind getting in trouble, now that I have a life that I love, I want to be able to keep it, which means not falling back into old habits.

"No, it's nothing like that," he assures me yet doesn't make any effort to explain further. "So, what do you think? Would you be willing to come home for a bit and help me with your mom's stuff?"

Part of me wants to say *no* because I honestly don't want to go. But I also don't want to be responsible for him doing this by himself then losing his shit and returning back to his old habits of drinking and doing drugs all day and night.

Damn conscience. It's getting on my nerves.

"I can probably do that, but I need to talk to Micha first," I tell him. "I'll call you tomorrow."

"Thanks, Ella." He sounds relieved.

"You're welcome."

We say our goodbyes then hang up.

"Okay, so what's up?" Micha asks as I hand him back his phone.

I waver. "How would you feel about me going home for a little bit? Or, well, back to Star Grove?" I correct myself.

Sure, Star Grove is where I lived while I was growing up, but Micha and I have owned a place in San Diego for quite a while. And I like it better there.

His brow arches. "Why?"

I give him a quick recap of what happened during the phone conversation.

"Wait. How did he get the money to pay the past due payments on the house?" he asks after I've finished telling him.

I shrug. "I'm not sure. He was super vague about it."

He rubs his scruffy jawline. "Sounds suspicious."

I nod in agreement. "I know."

He contemplates something. "Maybe you shouldn't go."

"I really don't want to," I admit. "But I kind of think I should."

I can tell he wants to argue, but he doesn't.

"Maybe I could bail on the next performance and fly back with you," he suggests, stroking my hip with his thumb.

I give him a firm look. "Your career is just starting to take off. There's no way I'm going to let you risk ruining that just so you can go back home with me for a few days. I can handle this. Besides, with this whole stalker thing going on, it might be good for me to get away."

"Right," he says with frown. "I actually kind of agree with you on that. I just wish you weren't going back to Star Grove. So much bad shit happened there."

I can't blame him for thinking that. "I know a lot of bad stuff happened there, but some good stuff, too," I remind him, skimming my fingertip along the ring on my ring finger.

"You're right. It did," he agrees, molding his fingers around my hips. Then he pulls me against him and kisses me deeply, sucking on my bottom lip before pulling back.

"I get to fuck you before you go, right?" His lips

are close enough that they brush mine.

I nod, shutting my eyes. "Just make sure the curtains are closed … and the computer is off." My stomach churns at the reminder of what happened.

He gives a brief pause. "I have a better idea." He stands up, carrying me with him as he heads into the bathroom. There, he strips my clothes off then his own before turning the shower on.

"I've had two showers already today," I tell him as my gaze skims across his lean chest, tattooed with lyrics he wrote for me a long time ago.

"Are you saying you don't want me to fuck you in the shower?" His brow teases upward. So does the corners of his lips.

He knows me too well, knows how much I like it in the shower.

One of the first times we were really intimate with each other was when we were in the shower together. Ever since, we've had a lot of shower sex in hotel rooms all over the country.

"No. That's not what I'm saying at all." I press my chest against his, loop my arms around the back of his neck, and kiss him.

He kisses me back, steering me into the shower, steam surrounding us.

A minute or so later, after we've touched and

kissed each other thoroughly, he's slipping inside me. And, for a moment, everything is perfect.

For a moment, everything seems like it'll stay that way.

But then we leave the shower and Micha receives the text. And just like that, the perfection shatters.

MICHA

I can't fucking believe this. I mean, I've heard horror stories of stalkers from other band members, but I never thought it'd be this bad. Truthfully, I didn't think I was popular enough to be dealing with this yet.

"I'm so sorry," I apologize to Ella as I pace the bedroom floor, holding the towel around my waist. "I'm so sorry, baby. I'm sorry."

"Will you stop apologizing?" She leaps off the bed and steps in front of me, stopping me from pacing, still wearing nothing but a towel herself. She'd been pretty quiet since we got out of the shower and saw that I had missed a message. I assumed it was from her dad or my manager, but nope. It was from her, the insane stalker who upped her crazy level with that text. It's from an unknown number, but it's pretty clear who sent it.

Unknown: Text me back or those photos and the video will be released to some pretty popular websites.

And just like that, that rage I felt earlier was back.

"This isn't your fault," Ella continues, drawing me out of my thoughts.

"It is, though," I disagree, raking my fingers through my damp hair.

"No, it's not." She sweeps a few strands of hair out of my eyes and looks up at me with nothing but love in her gaze. "And you're going to stop thinking that, or I'm never going to let you have sex with me again."

Even though I'm fuming, I have to bite back a smile. "I call bullshit. You like me between your legs just as much as I like being between your legs."

She crosses her arms, a challenge dancing in her eyes. "Are you playing chicken with me, Micha Scott?"

I bite down on my bottom lip. I fucking love it when she gets like this. "Yeah, I am Ella May Scott." Even after being married for a little bit, I still love saying her full name.

She considered hyphening her last name with mine, but then she decided she wanted to be a Scott more than a Daniels.

"You should know better than to play chicken with me," she warns haughtily.

She's probably right, but I'm kind of getting turned on right now, so I'm about to keep going. But then my phone vibrates with an incoming message.

I almost don't want to look, but the not knowing becomes too great for me.

Sighing in frustration, I stride over to the bed and grab the phone.

Unknown: I want a date with you, or else the video and photos will be all over the internet.

"This is blackmail," Ella whispers as she leans over my shoulder and reads the message.

"I know." I blow out a breath and turn toward her. "I don't know what to do."

"Well, you sure as hell are not going on a date with her."

"I know ... But what if she goes through with her threat?"

"I don't think she will. And besides, who the hell is she going to give the video and photos to that they'd end up all over the internet?"

"I don't know." I brush a strand of hair out of her beautiful green eyes. "But I don't want to risk it."

"And I don't want you risking going out on a date with someone who's clearly unstable. And trust me;

she is. I kind of went out on a date with her today, remember?" The corners of her lips tug downward.

I nibble on my lip ring. "So, what do you suggest we do?"

She shrugs, absentmindedly tracing her finger along my abs and causing me to shiver. "That officer gave you his card. Call and tell him. I know it probably won't do any good, but we should at least tell them what's going on."

"I guess so."

I don't like this feeling—this warning hanging over my head.

I've always had this urge to protect Ella, and that urge is currently swelling inside me.

While I wasn't thrilled about her going back to Star Grove, considering how much bad shit happened there, I'm starting to think that it might be for the best right now. At least until we can figure out this whole stalker situation. Because, while it's going to ache deep in my soul to not see her every day, at least with her so far away, I know she'll be far away from this mess.

At least I know she'll be safe.

I CALL the officer like Ella suggested, but he still doesn't act like there's much he can do. He says he'll add it to the report and to report any further information and incidents.

I hang up, feeling pretty frustrated.

Both Ella and I decide that she should probably fly out tomorrow so she can get away from all this immediately. Although she's a bit reluctant about it, I insist it's for the best, even though I'm going to miss her like hell.

I end up lying awake in bed for several hours. By the time the sun rises, I've barely gotten any sleep, my mind racing with ideas on how to stop this stalker.

Ella managed to pass out, though, and when she wakes up, she rolls over and blinks sleepily at me. It's one of my favorite looks on her.

She props up on her elbows as her gaze scans my face. "Did you sleep at all last night?"

I shake my head as I play with strands of her hair. "Not really."

"Is it because of the stalker?" she asks, sitting up. She's wearing one of my T-shirts, another look that I love on her. "Or because I'm leaving this morning?"

"Both," I admit, giving her a kiss. "How long do you think you'll be gone?"

"I'm not sure, but definitely not more than a week." She slips her leg over me so she's straddling me. "I don't think I can be away from you any longer than that. No matter what's going on." Then she dips her head to give me a deep kiss.

I cup the back of her head, holding her there, and she grinds her hips against mine.

Kissing her is always amazing, even when we both have morning breath.

"You're going to call me every hour, right?" I whisper after we break the lip lock.

She nods, her hair tickling my cheeks. "I'm picking up a new phone on my way to the airport. When I get to Star Grove, I'll take my computer in to get checked."

"I'm going to drive with you to the airport," I tell her, softly kissing her cheek and breathing in her scent.

She sits up. "I thought you had a meeting with Mike this morning?"

"Mike can wait," I tell her. "This—you—you're always the most important thing in my life."

"Micha …" she starts, but I silence her by sitting up and kissing her breathless.

"Nothing you can say will ever change that," I promise. "No matter what, pretty girl, you will always, *always* come first." Which is why I need to figure out how to stop this whole stalking thing, no matter what it takes. And then we can go back to living our life together.

I just hope this isn't going to become something that's a constant issue. If so, I'm not sure what the hell I'm going to do.

ELLA

EVEN THOUGH MICHA is blowing off his meeting with Mike and despite my protests, deep down, I'm glad he's going with me. I want to spend every moment I can with him.

We take a cab to the phone store, and then to the airport. By the time we arrive, I feel restless and worried about being away from Micha, about going home, about flying, about this stalker—I'm worried about a lot of things—but I hide it the best I can.

Micha, being Micha, senses my anxiety, though he seems distracted as I check into the flight, get my boarding pass, and check my suitcase.

"You want me to buy a boarding pass so I can go with you through security?" he offers as I step into the security line with him by my side. He's insisting he stay with me until the last minute, and I'm glad he is. I hate flying and airports. Always have.

I shake my head, clutching my boarding pass and ID in one hand. My purse is draped over my shoulder. "Don't be silly. That's a waste of money."

"You're nervous," he states the obvious, his eyes searching mine. "Not just about flying but about all of this."

"I know, but I can handle it," I assure him, looking him straight in the eyes so he knows I mean what I say.

I just hope that I do mean what I say—that I can handle this. I want to believe that I can, but going back home without Micha, without my safety net, is going to be a complication. However, I'm stronger than I used to be. I just need to remember that.

"I know you can, but I hate that you have to." He brushes his knuckles along my cheekbone, causing my eyelashes to flutter. "I wish I was going with you."

"I wish you were going with me, too," I murmur.

As the line moves forward, closer to the entrance, I know it's time to say goodbye.

I throw my arms around him, hugging so tightly I can barely breathe. "I love you."

He hugs me back just as tightly and breathes me in. "I love you, too, baby. Always have. Always will."

I love it when he says that.

And that's what I hold on to as I let him go and move forward to the security entrance.

Right before I walk through, I cast one final glance back at Micha.

He looks worried but hurriedly smiles, pretending everything is okay.

I want nothing more than to run back to him, but I know I can't. That is, unless I want to miss my flight. So, I smile back at him, pretending I'm okay, too, and hoping it alleviates some of his worry. Then I turn forward and walk, stepping through security before heading toward a flight that will take me back to Star Grove.

As I'm nearing my gate, my phone rings. Figuring it's Micah, I quickly dig it out of my pocket. It's not from Micha, though. It's from Lila.

"Hey," I answer as I make my way past people, steering my suitcase behind me.

"Hey." She sounds edgy, which is really weird for her.

"What's happened?" I ask as I reach the gate and skim the seating area for a vacant seat.

"What makes you think something happened?"

"Because I'm your best friend." I plop down in an empty seat and try to relax, but can't quite get there. "Plus, you sound nervous."

"I'm not," she replies way too quickly.

Someone says something in the background. It's a male voice but it's not Ethan's.

What the shit?

I'm about to ask her what's up, when she sputters, "Look, I have to make this call really quick. I'm in kind of a mess and need a place to lie low for a while. Would you and Micha mind if I came and crashed your roadtrip. It'd only be for like a week tops."

Okay, something's definitely up. "I'm actually headed back to Star Grove for the week. I'm at the airport right now."

"Oh." She grows quiet.

"You're welcome to come there, though," I tell her warily.

Not because I don't want her to come, but because Star Grove isn't really a place most people want to go. But Lila's been there before, so she's aware of how things are there.

"Yeah. Okay. I guess that works." She sounds a bit more relaxed now. That male voice says something again and she quickly tells me, "I have to go. But I'll text you when I'm on the road. I have to drive there because... Well, I just have to."

"Um, okay. You're acting really weird."

"I know." She sighs heavily. "I'll tell you why when I get to Star Grove. This isn't an over the phone conversation."

"Okay." I stand up as boarding is announced. "Is Ethan coming with you?"

"I'm not sure yet." That edginess creeps into her tone again. "Look, I really do have to go. Talk to you soon. And thanks in advance for letting me stay with you."

With that, she hangs up, leaving me to wonder what the heck is going on. But I guess I'll have to wait, at least until my flight is over. Because it's time to board the plane now.

Time for me to go back to Star Grove.

But right as I'm about to hand the attendant my boarding pass, I have this strange feeling I'm being followed. Worried maybe Crazy Stalker Pants is following me, I cast a quick glance over my shoulder. I don't see her anywhere, so I try to shove all thoughts aside and focus on boarding.

Focus on what I'm going to do when I get to Star Grove and return to my past.

MICHA

I HATE SEEING her walk away, though I know it's for the best. Still, I'm anxious during the drive back to the hotel. Part of me wishes I could've gone with her, but Ella is right. I need to continue the tour. I'm just glad that it's almost over. Not because I hate it, but because I'd like to have a little break, go home for a while, and just focus on Ella and me for a bit. And I want to get away from all this shit, like stalkers. Plus, Mike wants me to put out an album, which I'm so onboard for.

Speaking of Mike, I receive a message from him about halfway back to the hotel, chewing my ass out for missing the meeting this morning. When I tell him what's going on, he chills out a little. Let me stress the "little" part. The guy is kind of an asshole, but he seems to know what he's doing when it comes to the business and is a good manager.

As I'm getting out of the cab and heading into the hotel, I receive another message from him.

Mike: Let's meet up before we hit the road tonight.

I text back as I'm walking toward the entrance.

Me: Sounds good.

I start to put my phone away when I receive another text. I assume it's Mike again, but it's not. It's from the unknown number.

Unknown: So, do we have a deal?

Unknown: Stop ignoring me!

Unknown: I know you're reading these messages.

Unknown: Answer me!

Unknown: You're going to regret this!

The texts just keep coming through, one after another.

Unknown: Micha, I love you.

Unknown: You look so good in those jeans. I want to grab your ass. I'm just too nervous. Maybe if you tell me it's okay, that you want it. Do you want it? Do you want me?

Tension flows through my body as I stand in front of the hotel's entrance and peer over my shoulder, half-expecting her to be standing behind me. I can't see anyone nearby who looks suspicious or fits the description Ella gave me of the stalker, but I have the strangest feeling that I am being watched.

I hurry inside, preparing to head straight up to my room where I can lock the door and call the officer. Again. But, as I'm passing through the lobby, Elijah spots me from where he is hanging out in the lounge chairs with his band, calls out my name, and gets up, heading over to me.

I pause then turn around, putting on a fake smile, pretending everything is fucking okay.

"Hey," he says as he reaches me. "I just wanted to check in with you. You and Ella took off so quickly last night."

"Yeah, with all the stalker drama, we kind of just wanted to go back to the hotel," I admit, ignoring my buzzing phone.

Why the fuck won't she stop texting me?

I'm going to have to get my number changed or something.

Elijah glances down at my phone then back at me. "Is everything okay?"

I could lie, but Remi and him said that they'd been through a similar situation, so I decide to confide in him.

By the time I'm finished, I expect him to look surprised, but he doesn't.

As my phone goes off *again,* I grimace. "I just wish she'd fucking stop. Maybe she will when we leave Phoenix and I'm not by her anymore."

Wariness crosses Elijah's features as he stuffs his hands into his pockets. "Maybe. But don't count on it. More than likely, she'll probably follow you."

I shake my head in frustration then hit *silence* and pocket my phone. "What the hell am I supposed to do then? Because the cops act like there isn't much they can do and her—this stalker chick—said she'd only stop if I go out on a date with her."

"Don't do that," he says quickly. "Trust me. That'll only feed into her obsession more. Plus, depending on how intense she is, it could be dangerous."

I release an exhausted sigh. "Then, what am I supposed to do?"

He gives a glance around, which I find odd, then steps closer to me. "My advice would be to hire a PI who could track this girl down and find information on her. The more you know about her, the better. Plus, if she has a warrant out on her or something, you can get her put behind bars."

I nod, liking the idea. "That's actually a pretty good idea, but where do I find a PI that would do that?"

He stuffs his hand into his pocket, takes out his wallet, and digs a card out of it. "I used this guy a few of times. He resides in California, but he's willing to travel, and he's really cheap."

I wonder why he had to hire a PI multiple times. Because of stalkers?

I take the card from him. "Thanks. I think I'll give him a call."

"When you do, tell him his older brother says hi," he says, stuffing his wallet into his pocket.

My brow arches. "Your brother's a PI?"

He nods. "Yep, that's another reason why I know a thing or two about this stuff."

That makes sense, I guess.

His lips part, but then he closes his mouth as one of his band members calls out his name.

"I got to go help pack up some stuff," he tells me, backing away toward the lounge area. "But if you need a riding buddy during the drive tonight, let me know. Remi and I are cool with switching vehicles."

"Okay," I tell him, figuring I probably will since I'm tired as hell. Then I turn and head for the elevators to go up to my room.

I wait until I get there to call the PI, mostly because I'm a little uneasy over this feeling that I'm being followed and watched. Once I'm inside my room, I dial the number on the card. A secretary answers, takes all my info, and then informs me that Ryder will be in touch with me soon to discuss the details of the case further. By the time I hang up, I feel weird, restless, and frustrated.

When I decided to enter the music business, I hadn't given too much thought into this side of it. If I had, I may have been a bit hesitant about that decision. I mean, I love music and everything, but this sucks. If I were single, I wouldn't care as much. But when it involves Ella …

Yeah, I'm going to do whatever it takes to get this stalker out of our lives. And then, moving forward, I may have to rethink this whole music tour thing.

ELLA

So Star Grove is so small and secluded that there isn't a direct flight there. After I land, I have to rent a car and drive for about two hours. It's fine, though. Well, it wouldn't be that bad except snow is covering the mountains, trees, and forest—everything really. And the road is covered with ice. I already figured it'd be like this, though, so I rented a four-wheel drive SUV. Still, even though I'm an expert on driving on icy roads—having learned how to drive on them—when a blizzard rolls in and darkness begins to shadow the sky, I get a bit tense.

Flipping on my wiper blades, I squint against the near white-out as I steer around the windy road that weaves around the frozen lake. My grip on the steering wheel is tight and only tightens when the bridge comes into view.

That bridge holds so many memories, most of them awful, stemming from when I almost jumped to when I found my mom standing on the edge of it, telling me she could fly. Ethan had been the one to convince her to get down, something I'm grateful for, even if Ethan and I don't always get along.

Speaking of which...

I press Lila's number and put it on speakerphone, leaving my phone balanced on the console as I drive.

"Hey," she answers after three rings.

"Hey... How far away are you?"

"The GPS says I still have about five hours."

I frown at the winter wonderland in front of me. "You might want to pull over and stay at a hotel then. It's snowing so hard here I can barely see."

"Shit," she curses. "I was hoping to get there tonight, so I could finally just relax."

"You say that like you've been stressed out lately."

"I kind of have."

"Oh." I pause, wondering if I should ask the question that's been bothering me since she called me the last time. "Who was that guy I heard talking the last time you called."

She sighs heavily. "That would be Nico."

"Who the hell is Nico?"

"This guy Ethan knows... He let me borrow his car, so I could drive out there."

"Is Ethan with you?"

"No... But he might come out there in like a week or so."

"You're being super vague."

"I know." She sighs again. "Some stuff's going on, but I'd rather not talk about it while I'm on the phone with you. Tomorrow let's have lunch at that diner, and we can talk."

"Sounds good." I slow down for a turn. "Is everything okay between you and Ethan?"

"Yeah... Well, as good as it can be in this type of situation," she explains, being vague again.

"Now you've got me really interested."

"Well, it's a really interesting story."

"That you can't tell me over the phone."

"Yep, that I can't tell you over the phone."

Le sigh. She's got me really intrigued, but I guess I'll have to wait until tomorrow.

After that, we hang up, and I continue my snowy drive to Star Grove. The moment I enter the town, passing the faded sign that reads: *Welcome to Star Grove, Population 15,435*, a frown pulls at my lips. Every time I visit here, I do the same thing, not because I completely hate it. It's just that so much emotional stuff happened at this place, some things wonderful, while others downright awful. It also doesn't help that the town is run down, old, and has minimal amenities. However, it's the place Micha and I fell in love with, so even though it's kind of a shit hole, it'll always hold a special place in my heart.

Since blizzards are typical for Star Grove, a few people are driving around, although not as many as there would be. Not that there's a crap ton of traffic always clogging up the roads. In fact, I'm not sure I've ever had to deal with traffic while I was here.

No, the crap I have to deal with is totally family related. Sure, my dad has been nicer since he sobered up, but the baggage between us remains super heavy and painfully obvious, like a big old white elephant dancing in the room, totally butt ass naked.

Not that elephants typically wear clothes...

Not that that's even relevant right now...

But yeah, anyway...

Focusing on the road, I drive through the main section of town, which lasts about a minute tops. Then I keep driving, past the farmhouses, and railroad tracks until I reach the neighbor Micha and I grew up in.

The entire town may be outdated, but the area we were raised in is straight-up run down, the houses all looking broken, and the streets are covered in potholes. Some people are pretty decent that live around here, like Micha's mom, but some are sketchy to say the least. My dad and mom used to be those kinds of people.

Honestly, part of me doesn't even want to know about the stuff my parents have done, and I'm a little worried about what I'll find while helping my dad look through my mom's old stuff. I'm also a bit concerned about how he got the money to pay off all the overdue payments for the house. He was so vague about it, and while my dad may be doing better now, it's hard to forget all the cons he did while I was growing up. Not that I want to bring that up. If he is doing better, starting a fight with him could result in him falling off the wagon or something.

Deciding to keep quiet about it for now, I slow down to make a turn into the driveway of the small, two-story house that I grew up in. While my dad may have paid off the overdue payments, he apparently hasn't done any maintenance on the house; the siding is peeling off, a window is boarded up, and the front porch railing has tipped over. His Firebird isn't in the driveway either, which is a little bizarre since when I called him to say that I'd landed, he told me he'd be home when I arrived, and that he didn't have any plans of going anywhere.

Maybe he just ran to the store or something, I tell myself, trying to be optimistic as I can.

I park in the driveway near the fence that divides Micha's mom's house with my dad's property.

Then I shut off the engine, grab the keys, and hop out. I'm wearing boots, thankfully, since the snow is so deep that I sink all the way to my knees.

"Yep, seems about right," I mutter to myself as I tromp through the snow and to the back of the SUV.

Then I pop open the back, grab my bag, and hike up the driveway to the side door of the house. I don't bother knocking as I open up the door and step inside the kitchen. The lights are off in there, but light is flowing through the doorway that leads to the living room, so I can make out the countertops and the trash piled on them.

It looks just like it did when I was a kid.

I cringe at that thought, but decide to remain optimistic. Perhaps my dad just hasn't cleaned yet. He always has been sort of messy. Plus, he's single and works.

"Dad?" I call out as I set my bag down onto the kitchen table.

Nothing but silence, so I make my way into the living room. Then my jaw nearly smacks against the shaggy orange carpet. It looks like a tornado swept through here; boxes along with papers, photos, and several different items cover the floors, sofas, and coffee table.

"What the shit?" I pick up the closest item, which happens to be a photo of my mom sitting on the hood of my dad's firebird. It was back when she was pregnant with either Dean or me, her auburn hair is blowing in the wind, and she's smiling. But her eyes look shadowed over with sadness. A sadness that I now know had to do with depression.

As my chest tightens, I set the photo down. My gaze sweeps across the living room, and I seriously have no idea what to do.

"Dad?" I call out again, but receive the same answer of silence.

The house is actually eerily silent to the point that I'm starting to get the heebie-jeebies. That's why when my phone rings, shattering the silence, I nearly jolt out of my skin.

"Holy crap." I breathe heavily with my hand pressed against my chest. Then I dig my phone out of my pocket and see that it's Micha calling me. "Hey," I answer as I step over a box and head toward the stairway.

"Hey, baby," he says, the sound of his voice calming me just a smidgeon. "Did you get there yet?"

"Yeah, like five minutes ago. It's snowing pretty hard."

"I'm not surprised. You rented a four-wheel drive vehicle, though, right?"

"Of course. I'm not an amateur dude," I tease as I slowly make my way up the stairs.

Boxes are on the steps as well, some empty, some containing what looks like old clothes.

He chuckles. "Yeah, I guess not." He pauses for a beat. "So, how's everything going so far?"

I step over a box blocking the top of the stairway. "It's only been like five minutes."

"A lot can happen in five minutes, Ella May," he says in all seriousness. "Especially when your father is involved."

"You're worried about me," I state as I flip on the hallway light and frown at the sight of yes, you guessed it, more boxes.

"Of course I'm fucking worried about you. I hate that you're there without me... I should be there."

"Micha, I can handle being here for a week by myself," I insist.

Although, when I reach my dad's bedroom, I question if maybe I can't.

Inside, the room is fucking trashed, clothes scattered everywhere, along with cigarette butts and cans of what I'm hoping is soda.

"Jesus," I mutter, shaking my head at the mess.
And the stench.

"What's wrong?" Micha asks immediately.

Not wanting to worry him, I almost don't tell him.

But we made a vow a bit ago not to keep stuff from each other.

"The house is a mess," I answer as I step inside the room and pick up one of the cans.

Surprisingly, it is soda, but that doesn't explain the mess.

"Isn't that sort of normal?" Micha asks.

"This is beyond the usual messy normal," I say, scratching at my head. "There's garbage everywhere and boxes. And all the stuff from the boxes is scattered all over the house." I bend down and pick up another photo; this one of my mom and dad standing in front of the house. "I think my dad may have gone through my mom's stuff without me."

"Shit, really?" More worry fills Micha's voice.

"Yeah, I think so." I set the photo down and step out of the room, turning off the light behind me. "I don't know why he'd do that after he asked me to come out here and help him go through the boxes."

"Maybe he just started without you."

"Maybe." I glance around and frown. "I don't know, though, it kind of looks like he was looking for something."

"Did you ask him about it?"

"No. But only because he's not here."

"Where do you think he is?"

I head toward my old bedroom. "Well, normally,

I'd say at the closet bar, but he's sober now, and I have no idea where my sober dad hangs out." It's the truth, too.

My dad has been a drunk way longer than he's been sober to the point that I feel like I really don't know anything about him anymore.

"Maybe my mom knows where he is?" he suggests. "You want me to call her?"

"Nah, I can just go over there and ask her. I saw her car in the driveway when I pulled up so she should be home," I say, stepping into my room and flipping on the light.

Holy freakin' memories.

My dad never did anything with my room, so all of my old drawings and sketches are still taped to the purple walls that Micha and I painted. My bed is unmade, and some of my art supplies are scattered across it. What really gets to me, though, is the guitar propped up in the corner. It was one of Micha's first guitars, and he used to spend hours in my room playing songs he wrote while I sketched.

"Is everything okay?" he asks worriedly. "You just got really quiet."

"Everything's fine." I make my way over to the guitar and pluck a few strings. "I just walked into my room, and it's like a floodgate of memories crashed over me at once."

"You're not getting overwhelmed, are you?"

"No... The memories that happened in here are mostly good."

"True." He pauses, and when he speaks again, hilarity rises in his tone. "I remember the first time I saw your nipples, we were in your room."

"Hey," I protest, sinking onto the edge of the bed. "That's so not true. The first time I was shirtless in front of you, we were in your bedroom."

"Yeah, but that wasn't the first time I saw your nipples. The very first time it happened was when you left your bedroom curtain open while you were changing."

"There's no way you could've seen my nipples all the way over from your house."

"I got a decent look, but the first time I got an eyeful was that one time I showed up at your house, and you were wearing that white tank top without a bra."

I laugh softly. "I remember that. I was so embarrassed, but I pretended just to be pissed off at you."

"I know. You threw a pillow at me," he says with a soft chuckle. "It didn't really matter, though. You could've thrown anything at me, and it would've been worth it. I was so turned on."

I roll my eyes. "Only because you were a horny teenage boy."

"That might've been part of it," he agrees. "But you were also so fucking hot. Seriously, I already thought you were gorgeous before then, but after that, I realize how much I wanted you. In fact, I dreamt about fucking you that night."

"Good lord," I groan, lying back on the bed. "I take back what I said earlier. You weren't a horny teenage boy. You are a horny guy, like all the time."

"Only because I have the hottest wife ever."

"You're crazy."

"So? You love my crazy."

"Maybe just a little bit."

He chuckles, his laughter quickly fading. "Have you headed over to my mom's house yet?"

"No. I'm lying down in my bed. I'll head over in a few." I flick a glance at the window where snow flurries are tumbling from the sky. "I want to see if the snow will let up."

"Good luck with that," he snorts, the sound of laughter rising in the background

"Hey, it doesn't hurt to try." I flip over on my stomach. "Where are you? I suddenly hear a bunch of background noise."

"I'm at a restaurant with some of the bands," he explains. "We're still on the road, but everyone was getting hungry."

"How's the driving by yourself going?"

"It's not too bad. I miss you, though."

"I miss you too." I sit up, raking my fingers through my hair. "It was probably good to leave Phoenix, though, right? So at least you'll be away from crazy stalker girl." He doesn't answer right away, causing nervousness to spike through me. "Is everything okay?"

"Just a second," he says quietly, and the background noise slowly dwindles. "I didn't want to talk about this where everyone can overhear."

"Did something happen?"

"Kind of." He blows out a sigh. "She texted me a few times after I dropped you off at the airport. At first, I just sort of ignored it, but then it became pretty clear that she was watching me and might be a bit obsessed with me."

I worry my lip between my teeth. "How do you know she was watching you?"

"Just some of the stuff she said made it pretty clear," he replies vaguely, probably trying to protect me. "It's okay, though. I hired a PI to look into it."

"Seriously?"

"Yeah. I mean, I know it kind of sounds crazy, but I think it's better to be safe, right?"

"Yeah, I guess." I give a short pause. "You think she's going to follow you?"

"I don't know. She might."

"That's... creepy."

"I know. But like I said, I'm having a PI look into it, so hopefully, we'll find out who she is."

"And then what?" I ask. "And how did you even find a PI?"

"It's actually Elijah's older brother."

"Elijah's brother is a PI?"

"Apparently."

"Well, that's kind of cool and very convenient for us."

"I know. And I think this'll go better than with the police since we're paying him to look into it."

"I see your point and everything, but what're we going to do when we find out who she is? I mean, it's not like the police seem that eager to do anything."

"I'm not sure yet, but I'll ask Ryder."

"Ryder?"

"That's the PI's name."

"Oh." I crinkle my nose. "This is so weird. I mean, PI's? Stalkers? And this cold case with my mom."

"I know." He gives a short pause. "Baby, if you need me to come there, I can."

"No way," I tell him as I stand up from the bed. "I already said I'm not going to let you leave the tour. You're doing your dream, Micha, and there's no way I'm going to let you give that up." I square my shoulders, mostly to make myself feel more confident. "I can handle this."

He doesn't answer right away. "Okay. But if you need anything at all, call me, even if it's in the middle of the night."

"That goes for you too," I tell him as I head out of my room. "And keep my updated on this PI/Stalker thing."

"I will," he vows, and the background noise gets louder. "My foods at the table. I gotta go, but call me in the morning, okay."

"Okay. Love you."

"Love you too, pretty girl."

We hang up, and I start checking the house for more clues as to what in the world my dad was doing and where he could be. Ultimately, though, I get nowhere, so I dig my coat out of my suitcase and head over next-door to talk to Micha's mom.

Back in the day, I'd just walk in, but without Micha living there, it seems weird. So instead, I knock, my breath coming out into a cloud of smoke.

It takes a couple of knocks before Micha's mom opens the door. As soon as she sees me, a big smile consumes her face.

"Hey," she greets me. "I didn't know you guys were visiting. I thought the tour was still going." She looks over my shoulder, probably looking for Micha.

"Actually, it's just me," I inform her, pulling my coat tighter around myself. "Micha's still on tour."

Worry suddenly floods her features. "Is everything okay with you two?"

I nod. "Yeah, everything's fine. I just came here for a week because my dad needed help with something." I leave out the part about the stalker, figuring Micha can tell her about it if he wants to. "That's actually why I came over here to see if you know where my dad is?"

She shakes her head. "Sorry, sweetie, but I don't. I've been gone a lot, though, this week because I've been taking some extra shifts at work."

"Oh." I try not to frown but fail epically. "When's the last time you've seen him?"

"About a week ago." She points to the garage. "He was hauling boxes in from there."

That's odd since he just called me a few days ago to ask me to come help him look through the boxes. Why did he haul them all inside and then go through them without my help if he asked for my help? It doesn't make any sense.

"You want to come inside for a bit?" she asks me. "I just made some cookies."

"I think I need to go find my dad first and let him know I'm here," I tell her. "Can I stop by tomorrow, though?"

She nods with a smile. "Of course, Ella. You're my daughter-in-law—you're always welcome here."

I smile back as I back off the porch. "Okay, see you tomorrow."

She waves at me as I walk away, hiking through the snow and back toward the fence. "And let me know if you need anything!" she calls out.

I nod, then she shuts the door while I hoist myself over the fence. Once I get on the other side, I start up the driveway toward the garage to see if maybe my dad is in there. When I step inside, my jaw nearly smacks the concrete ground.

All the shelves are almost empty. In fact, the only thing in there is a trunk, along with a few trash cans, and a lamp.

"What the fuck?" I mutter, scratching my head.

I mean, I know my dad hauled those boxes inside, but why? Why take everything inside. Well, except for this trunk. He left that out here for God knows what reason. And what the hell is even in it?

Rubbing my lips together, I make my way over there. I have no idea why I'm so nervous. It's just a trunk. That's all. But I can't help thinking about all those years ago when my mom was a suspect in that case and how for a while I actually questioned if she had something to do with it.

Exhaling shakily, I flip the latch and lift the lid.

When I see what's inside. I'm not sure if I should be relieved or worried. Because the trunk is empty.

"Seriously, what the actual fuck," I mumble as I close the lid.

Then I make my way inside, trying to figure out what to do next. I decide to call my dad, but it goes straight to voicemail, which means he either has it powered down or the battery is dead. I could go look for him, but like I said, I'm not sure where my sober dad is. Then again, maybe he fell off the wagon.

"Stop being so pessimistic, Ella," I say to myself as I stomp my feet off before walking inside the house.

I check the time. It's late enough that I'm starting to get kind of tired, especially after flying and driving all day. After thinking about it for a bit, I decide to just leave my dad a voicemail that I'm here, am going to bed because I'm tired and that I'll see him tomorrow. Then I go upstairs, get into my pajamas, and change the sheets and blankets on my bed before climbing in to go to sleep, hoping by tomorrow my dad will be here. And he'll be sober and have a good explanation for why the house is in so much disarray.

I'd be lying, though, if I said I wasn't worried.

MICHA

IT'S crazy that it's only been a little over a day, and I'm already missing her so badly I can't sleep for most of the night. Even before Ella and I started dating, we slept in the same bed a lot of nights, so not having her beside me feels strange and leads to a bad case of sleep insomnia. By the time morning rolls around, I feel strung out and exhausted.

Once I shower and get dressed, I head down to the lobby of the hotel we arrived at last night to go to the coffee shop. On my way out, I dial Ella's number, but she doesn't answer. She could very well still be asleep, but after talking to her last night, I'm a bit worried, mostly that her dad is drinking again. I didn't say it over the phone, though, not wanting to worry her. But that doesn't mean I'm not worried myself.

JESSICA SORENSEN

On a positive note, though, I haven't heard from the stalker, so I'm hoping that means maybe she couldn't leave Arizona. Not that I'm just going to let this go. With her having that photo of Ella and I having sex, I still need to hire the PI who can hopefully figure out who she is so we can get the video and put the stalking to an end. Although, I actually haven't received a call back from him yet. I'd be a bit concerned about that, but since this guy is Elijah's brother, I'm giving him the benefit of the doubt.

Then, as if he's read my mind, my phone rings, the call is from Ryder's office.

"Hello?" I answer as I leave my room and walk down the hallway toward the elevators.

"Hey, this is Ryder from the office of Delovonte's Investigations. I received your message. I also got a call from my brother, Elijah about you."

"Oh, okay, cool." I press the elevator button, but then realizing I'll lose service on it, turn and head for the stairway.

"He told me a little bit about you having an issue with a stalker," Ryder continues on. "But I'd like to get all of the details from you."

"Okay." I push through the doorway and start down the empty stairwell, giving him a quick recap of what's going on.

Once I'm done, he gives me a price for the job, and

114

it seems reasonable, but I think he might be giving me a discount because I know Elijah. The conversation takes a while to get through as he proceeds to ask me a lot of questions and gives me a rundown of what he'll be doing. Since I don't want to have this conversation in the lobby, I linger in the stairwell.

"So you're going to start in Arizona?" I ask once Ryder is wrapping up the conversation.

"Yeah. I figure it's the best place to start since that's where the stalking started and seemingly ended." He gives a short pause, and I can hear the clicking of keyboard keys. "However, I'm going to message you my private number, and if at any time they get a hold of you, I want you to call me and give me an update of what happened."

"Okay." My chest is starting to feel a bit tight as the stress of the situation crashes over me.

I'm usually good at handling stress, but this feels like an entirely new level of it.

I take a few deep breaths and lean against the railing. "So what're the odds of you being able to find this person?"

"Honestly, it all really depends on how bold they are," he answers. "If they continue to harass you, it'll be easier to catch them."

"So, you're saying it's better if they continue to harass me?"

"Kind of."

I exhale loudly. "All right, well, I'll make sure to keep you updated then."

"Thanks. And if you have any questions at all, just call me on the private number I'll be messaging you."

"Thanks."

We hang up, and I lower my head and pinch the brim of my nose. This is so fucking stressful, and truthfully, I just want to go back to Star Grove, be with Ella, and take a break from this. I know I'm supposed to be finishing the tour, and this is my dream and everything, but I'm not going to be able to enjoy it with this cloud of fucking stress hovering over me.

Taking a deep breath, I try calling Ella again, but she doesn't answer. Blowing out a sigh, I push against the handle of the door to exit the stairway. But weirdly, it's locked. Or stuck, since it budges a little.

"What the hell?" I push on the door again, but it doesn't open.

Grimacing, I head upstairs, feeling a pissy mood emerging. I need coffee. I need sleep. I need Ella.

I decide to send her a text, just a simple: *hey, call me when you wake up.* Then I stuff my phone into my back pocket and force myself to hurry my ass up the stairs. I'm about halfway up when I hear the door above open and shut. Footsteps come down the stairway, but only for a moment before they grow quiet.

Weird.

"Hey, whoever's up there, the door at the bottom is locked, so you might want to use the elevators," I call out.

A beat of silence ticks by, and then a soft giggle echoes down the stairway.

Okay, so I know a giggle probably doesn't sound scary, but when you're in a fucking stairway by yourself with the only accessible door locked, it's a bit eerie. Even eerier is when a deep laugh follows the giggle.

I grip the railing, frozen in place, and trying to figure out what the hell my next move is. I mean, it could just be a couple of giggly weirdos up there or clowns...

Clowns, Micha? Are you fucking serious right now?

"Hello?" I ask, pulling my phone out.

Another giggle.

Another laugh.

"You've got to be shitting me," I mutter, turning and descending back down the stairway as I dial Elijah's number.

"Hello?" he answers after a few rings, thankfully he sounds awake.

"Hey, can you come let me out of the stairwell?" I ask, knowing I probably sound weird.

"Um... sure?" He sounds as confused as he probably should. "Did you get locked in there?"

"Sort of," I reply vaguely. "Look, I'll explain more when you let me out."

"Okay. I'll head over now."

"Thanks," I say as I reach the bottom of the stairway. "And can you let me out from the one on the lobby floor."

"Sure..." He's so puzzled right now, and if I were in his position, I probably would be too.

"Thanks. I owe you one."

We hang up, and I wait near the door, continually checking to see if it's unlocked. The stairwell has grown really quiet to the point where I'm questioning if perhaps the gigglers went back up and exit through another door.

I just start to relax when I hear a clinking noise. A handful of seconds later, a swoosh reverberates through the air above me. I glance up just in time to see something tumbling toward me and have barely enough time to jump back before it lands on me. The object crashes against the floor with a loud clank as my back slams against the wall.

I pant for air, barely able to get oxygen into my lungs as I stare down the small metal trunk in front of me. It's not huge but definitely heavy enough that from the distance it fell, I could've gotten really hurt. Or worse.

Then I hear the giggle and laughing and see red. I'm about one step away from running up the stairs and beating some ass when the door beside me opens up.

Elijah pops his head in. "Hey, did you..." He trails off as he takes in the sight of my face and then the trunk in front of me. "What the hell happened?"

"That's what I'd really like to know." I flick a glance up at the stairway above, the air quiet again.

My phone buzzes from inside my pocket, and I take it out.

Unknown: Did you get my present?

My gaze drops to the trunk then I look at Elijah.

"So, I'm pretty sure the person stalking me is in this stairwell and just threw that at me." I point at the trunk.

His eyes widen. "Seriously?"

I nod. "Yep. I just got a text."

We exchange a look, and both silently agree to head back up the stairs and find the fuckers.

"There's two of them too," I explain to him as we rush up the stairs.

"How do you know that?"

"Because I heard two people giggling."

He slightly stumbles. "Giggle?"

"Oh, yeah, I forgot to mention that part. There was giggling from up above before that trunk got tossed at me." I quicken my pace, taking the steps two-by-two.

"This is fucking crazy," he mumbles. "Especially since the door wasn't locked. It was jammed on purpose."

"So this is a setup?" And if that's the case, then it means I'm being watched closely.

Rage simmers in my chest and only swells when I reach the top of the stairs and don't find anyone. I peer out into the hallway and find it empty.

"Son of a bitch." I step back into the stairway with my fists balled and shaking my head. "There's no one out there."

"Maybe the hotel has security cameras," he suggests, although he sounds doubtful.

I'm pretty doubtful too. And honestly, I really need a break from all of this.

"Let's go to the front desk and ask," he says, then starts down the stairway.

I follow, on edge, and feeling like I'm about to crawl out of my skin.

And that feeling only amplifies when I reach the bottom of the stairs where the trunk is.

"What's in it?" Elijah asks, staring at the trunk.

"I have no idea." I crouch down, peer inside, and lift the lid.

Then instantly regret doing so.

Inside the trunk are a few photos of Ella's mom, which is creepy in itself. But what's even worse is the person in the photos with her.

And the man is from the cold case currently being investigated. The one Ella's mom was, and maybe still is, a suspect in.

ELLA

I SLEEP LIKE CRAP, partly because my dad didn't come home early morning and partly because Micha isn't lying beside me. When I finally do fall asleep, it's not too long after I hear my dad come in. He's loud enough that I know it's him. He even calls out my name. But I swear I can hear a slight slur in his voice, and because of that, I don't answer—don't want to deal with what it probably means.

Eventually, I doze off and sleep well into the hours of late afternoon. And I only wake up because my phone is buzzing like crazy. Rolling over, I pick it up off my nightstand, blinking a few times and clearing out the sleepiness from my eyes as I answer.

"Hello?"

"Hey." Lila's voice flows through the line. "I'm at

your house... Did you know your front door was open? I mean, the screen is closed, but the actual door is wide open. And it's snowing!"

Her very much awake attitude yanks me from my sleepy daze.

"I didn't know it was open, but sometimes it doesn't shut all the way, and the wind blows it open." Which is true, but the reality is more than likely my dad stumbled in drunk at the butt crack of dawn and left it open. "And dude, you seriously have way too much energy for me right now."

"Oh. Yeah. Sorry. I drank like three cups of coffee this morning."

"Well, you're wired." I throw the covers off of me and rub my eyes with my free hand. "I'll come down and let you in through the side door."

"You don't just want me to come in through the open front door?"

"No. Trust me. There's some stuff going on... And it's just better if you walk through the side door." Because I'm fairly certain my dad's passed out on the sofa in the living room where the front door is.

"Okay." She sounds a little bit confused, but not completely.

Lila knows enough about me, though, that she might be able to put two and two together.

We hang up, and I pull on a pair of pants and a T-shirt before heading downstairs. The moment I reach the bottom floor, a massive wave of cold air crashes over me. My breath fogs out in front of my mouth, and goosebumps sprout across my arms.

I hurry to the side door and let Lila in.

"Holy crap, it's freezing," she chatters as she rushes inside, snow falling off her boots and snowflakes dotting her blond hair. She's wearing jeans and a jacket, along with a pair of fingerless gloves. Back in the day, she'd wear really preppy outfits that weren't made for winter. But then she reinvented herself and has gotten a little bit better.

"Yeah, winters here last a freakin' long time," I say as I shut the door behind her.

She wraps her arms around herself, her gaze skimming across the messy kitchen. "What happened here?"

"I honestly have no idea. I showed up last night and this was here."

"It looks like your dad's moving."

"He's not. Or well, as far as I know he's not."

She gives another glance around before looking at me. Then a smile breaks across her face as she goes right into happy Lila mode.

"I'm so excited to see you." She wraps her arms around me, giving me a hug. "It's been way too long."

I laugh softly as I awkwardly hug her back. "It's been like two months."

"That's a long time in friend land," she assures me, stepping back, her smile fading slightly. "I just wish I didn't have to come here under these kinds of circumstances."

"Yeah, are you gonna tell me why you're here? Not that I'm not excited you are, but you were super vague about the why."

She chews on her bottom lip while peering around nervously. "Can we talk about this in your room, maybe? It's kind of a private conversation."

"You're worrying me."

"Sorry."

The fact that she doesn't try to say I shouldn't be worried makes me even more anxious. "Let's go talk in my room then."

As we start toward the stairway, the air grows chiller, reminding me that I haven't checked on my dad or closed the front door.

"Go ahead and go up," I tell Lila as I stop and turn for the doorway. "I'm gonna go shut the door and check on my dad. I'll be up in a second."

Nodding, she hurries up the stairs while I step into the living room. As soon as I do, the smell of booze and cigarettes wafts over me. I smash my lips together as I make my way further into the room and close the front door. Then I turn toward the sofa where my father is sprawled out, empty bottles of beer scattered across the floor just below him. The ashtray on the coffee table is overflowing with cigarette butts.

As I stand there, staring at the mess in front of me, a wave of disappointment crashes over me. I know that I've dealt with my dad's alcoholism in the past, but now that he's been sober for a while, it's difficult to see him like this again.

But what happened between the time that he called me and now? Because as far as I could tell, he sounded sober on the phone.

"Ella?" My dad blinks his bloodshot eyes open at me.

By the dazed look on his face, I can tell he's still a bit drunk.

"Yeah, it's me." I nudge a few boxes out of my way and pad over to the sofa. "Are you okay?"

"No," he whispers drunkenly, his eyelids lowering.

I figure he means he's not okay because he fell off the wagon. That is until he mutters, "I lost the box, Ella. It's gone."

My brows knit. "What box?"

"The box with the photos... and the stuff with your mom... the stuff with that guy..." he murmurs, dozing off again.

"What stuff?" I ask.

When he doesn't answer, I softly shake him, but all he does is let out a loud snore, leaving me to wonder what stuff he can't find of my mom's and why it's so important that he slipped up on his sobriety over it.

ELLA

By the time I get up to my room, I'm frustrated and worried. But I force myself to be a good friend and shove my worries aside for a moment as I walk into my room and close the door behind me. Lila is on my bed when I enter, hugging a teddy bear of mine and staring off into empty space with a haunted look on her face.

Something terrible is going on, I think to myself as I make my way over to the bed and sit down beside her.

"What happened?" I ask, crisscrossing my legs and sitting in front of her.

She blows out an audible exhale as she looks at me. "It's bad, Ella. Like really bad." She swallows hard. "You have to promise me that what I'm about to tell you stays between us. I mean, you can tell Micha because I'm sure Ethan will, but no one else can know, okay?"

My heart is hammering in my chest as I nod. "You know I'm not one for gossip."

"I know. It's one of the many reasons why I love you." She offers me the most depressing looking smile ever. "Ethan and I... we saw someone murdered."

Okay, that so wasn't what I was expecting her to say.

"What?" I gape at her, waiting for her to say she's just kidding or something, but all she does is give an uneven nod.

"I can't get into all of the details right now, but this person that murdered them... They're really powerful, and if they found out Ethan and I saw what they did, we'd be..." She drags her finger across her throat and then bursts into tears.

I scoot forward and wrap my arms around her, trying to comfort her and trying not to freak out.

"I'm so scared," she sobs as she sinks into me. "Ethan says it's going to be okay because no one knows we know, but I can't stop thinking about how if we saw this guy get murdered, then maybe someone saw us. And I know Ethan's more worried than he's letting on because he suggested we come here for a while until this all blows over."

"I'm sure he's just being careful," I try to reassure her while patting her back.

Honestly, though, I'm super concerned myself. Ethan isn't much of a worrier, so if he's suggesting Lila and him hide out in Star Grove for a while, things have got to be bad.

"Where is Ethan anyway?" I wonder. "I mean, why didn't he drive here with you?"

"He said he had to take care of a few things," she whispers. "I don't know what he's doing, though, and I'm worried he did something stupid."

"Have you heard from him?"

She bobs her head up and down then leans away from me, sniffling. "He called me this morning and said he was headed out here."

"Well, then I'm sure everything is okay," I offer, hoping I'm right. "You want to call him and see? Maybe it'll make you feel better."

She nods again, drying her eyes before digging her phone out of her pocket. "That's a good idea." She gets up and moves over to the window to call him.

When she starts talking to him, I let out a breath of relief.

And I thought Micha and I have stuff to worry about. Sure, having a stalker is bad, but what Lila and Ethan are going through is beyond terrifying. And I don't even have all the details about it. I probably should get her to open up to me a little bit more just so I have a bigger idea of what's going on, seeing as how she's going to be staying with me. I should also warn her about my dad and this cold case. And I think I should call Micha and give him a heads up about this, and so he can call Ethan. When I look at my phone, though, I realize I'd been so distracted by Lila that I've missed a few calls and a text from him.

Lila is chattering away with Ethan, so I step out into the hallway to call Micha.

"Hey," he answers. "You finally called me back. I was starting to get worried."

"Yeah, sorry. I didn't fall asleep basically until the sun was coming up."

"Why? Did something happen? Or did you just miss me too much?" He's trying to be playful, but I detect the slightest bit of worry in his tone.

I sigh. "My dad came home drunk."

"Aw, baby, I'm so fucking sorry."

"It's okay. I just don't know why it happened. I mean, he sounded fine on the phone when I talked to him." I chew on my thumbnail. "I'm worried something bad happened. Maybe with this cold case, because when I went to check on him a couple of minutes ago, he was muttering something about losing a box that had some photos and stuff of my mom's and some guy's. He sounded really upset about it, but he's still drunk, so I'm not really sure." When he doesn't answer right away, I think maybe the call was dropped. "Are you there?"

"Yeah, I just..." He heaves a loud exhale. "So, I'm about five minutes away from your house, and there's some stuff I need to tell you, but I want to do it when I get there."

"What!" I exclaim. "Why are you in Star Grove? What about the performance tonight?

"I took a leave of absence," he informs me.

"Micha, you didn't need to do that," I tell him. "I said I could handle this."

"I know, but that's not the complete reason why I decided I needed to take a break from the tour."

Worry courses through my veins. "Did something else happen with the stalker?"

"Kind of." He pauses, being extremely evasive for him. "Give me a few minutes, and I'll be there, and I can explain everything."

"Fine. But FYI, Lila made it here already."

"Is Ethan there?"

"No, but you should probably call him," I say, then lower my voice and give him a quick recap of what Lila told me.

By the time I'm finished telling him, all he can say is, "Holy crazy shit."

"Yeah, it's definitely crazy," I agree. "And I think

you should call Ethan and make sure he's okay. I mean, Lila's talking to him right now, but it might be good for you to check in on him too."

"I definitely will, but I want to talk to you first... I'm pulling up in the driveway right now. Or well, my mom's driveway. Meet me at the fence, okay?"

I nod, even though he can't see me. "I'm headed down now."

Then I hang up and practically jog out of the house. I'll admit that while I like to pretend I can handle anything by myself, the amount of relief I feel when I see him and know I don't have to deal with this alone is almost indescribable.

He smiles at me as he climbs out of the car, but he looks exhausted; dark circles reside under his eyes, and strands of his hair are sticking up all over the place.

"I'm so damn glad to see you," he says as we both start toward the fence.

When we reach it basically at the same time, I begin to climb over. But he reaches over, grips my hips, and lifts me up, not setting me down, but urging me to fasten my legs around his waist. Once I do, he kisses me so deeply that for a brief moment, I forget about all of our problems.

"God, I missed you," he murmurs, his lips hovering over mine.

"We've only been apart for like twenty-four hours," I tease.

"And that's twenty-four hours too much," he says, his breath fogging out in front of him.

"It really is," I agree, then seal my lips to his.

We kiss for a few minutes before reluctantly breaking the kiss. Then he lowers me to the ground, the dazed look in his eyes morphing into worry. "There's something I need to show you."

"You look worried," I state as he threads his fingers through mine.

"I am a little bit," he admits. "I mean, I was already a bit worried before you called me, but after what you told me on the phone... About what your dad said..." He trails off, nervously sucking on his lip ring. "The stalker left something for me this morning. Or well, threw it at me."

I gape at him. "*Threw* it at you?"

"Yeah, when I was going down a stairwell they tried to lock me in..." He shakes his head and frowns. "It's a long story, and I'll tell you all the details, but first, I need you to come look at what's inside the trunk that they threw at me."

He threads his fingers through mine and guides me toward his car. I gulp shakily as he opens the door and grabs a small looking trunk from off the

passenger seat. The look on his face is pure nervousness, which is making me nervous.

"You're making me nervous," I tell him as I reach
toward the latch.

"I'm sorry. What's in there, though..." Snowflakes
dot his face as he chews on his bottom lip. "Just know
I'm here for you, and whatever you want to do with
this, I'll support that decision."

My stomach burns with uneasiness as I open the
latch of the trunk and peer inside. And just like that, I
understand why he looks so worried. Because inside
are photos of my mom and the guy she was once
accused of murdering.

ELLA

"YOU SAID the stalker threw this at you?" I ask as I close the trunk and glance up at Micha.

He nods, setting the trunk back down onto the passenger seat. "I have no clue how they got them, though."

"They... You think there's two of them?"

"Maybe. I mean, I heard two people in the stairway giggling and laughing before that trunk was dropped on me."

I lift a brow. "Giggling?"'

He nods uneasily. "Yeah, it was pretty crazy."

"Sounds like it," I mumble, trying to process everything he just told me. "Did you call the cops?"

He shakes his head, carrying my gaze. "I was worried about what would happen with the cold case if they saw these photos. I did call Ryder and tell him what happened, minus the photos, and he decided to skip investigating in Arizona for now, and head straight to the hotel I was staying in when this happened."

"What about the tour? Aren't you going to get into trouble for bailing out early."

"Mike wasn't thrilled about it," he admits. "But considering the circumstances, there was a safety concern, and he kind of had to let me leave."

Guilt weighs on my shoulder. "But you're missing your last few performances."

"Baby, I don't care about that." He places his hands onto my waist. "What I care about is that clearly there's some fucking whack job out there that's been stalking us for probably longer than we realized. And they've been to your father's house." He gives a contemplative pause. "Did you know about those photos?"

I shake my head. "No... I mean, I know my mom knew the guy as our neighbor, but clearly, she knew him better than I was aware of." My lips curve into a frown. "I wonder if my dad knows—if this is the missing stuff he was looking for." And I wonder what he was planning on doing with it if he found them. Would he have turned them over to the detectives working the cold case? Or destroyed them?

I'm not sure, but what I do know is I need to talk to him right now. I don't care if he's hungover. I need answers.

"I'm going to go talk to him about it." I turn and tromp through the snow, back toward the fence.

Micha grabs the trunk off the seat and follows after me. "You think it's a good idea to talk to him about this while he's hungover?"

"No. But I'm going to anyway." I grip the fence and hoist myself over it. "Because waiting is going to drive me crazy." I take the trunk from him so he can climb over the fence too.

"I just worry he'll be an asshole," he says, his worry written all over his face.

"I can handle my dad being an asshole," I assure him. "Because I have you now, and I don't have to deal with it alone."

I move toward the driveway, but he captures my hand and tows me back toward him.

"I fucking love you," he breathes out, then kisses me briefly yet deeply. "And yes, you do have me. Always. Don't forget that, pretty girl."

"I won't," I promise him, brushing my lips against his one time before stepping back.

Then we cross my driveway with our fingers interlocked and step into the house.

Micha's eyes widen as he scans the messy clutter

in the kitchen. "Holy shit, this place is even messier than it used to be, which is saying a lot."

"I know. I seriously thought that for a second he'd lied about catching up on the mortgage and was moving out."

"It looks like he is."

"I think he was looking for this." I lift the trunk up. "And after seeing what's in it, I'm now wondering what he planned on doing with it once he found it. Although, I'm not even sure how he knew it existed since him and my mom always acted like she barely knew the guy that was killed. At least that's what she always told the police. My parents have always been liars, though, which makes me question if he'll even be truthful about this when I show him."

"We don't have to show him," he stresses. "We can just leave it here and go stay over at my house. Let him deal with this mess."

"I wish it was that easy, but now that I've seen what's in this trunk, I want answers." Squaring my shoulders, I march into the room where my dad is sleeping, only to find him sitting up and smoking a cigarette.

His eyes are bloodshot, and he looks like he's about to barf all over the floor. When he looks at me, a drop of remorse flickers in his eyes but fades into confusion as he sees the trunk I'm holding.

He stumbles to his feet and rushes over to me, smoke circling the air. "Where did you find that?"

"It's a long story, but—" He snatches the trunk from my hands, storms over to the coffee table, and opens the lid of the trunk.

Then with a shaky breath, he drops the lit cigarette into the trunk, right on top of the photos.

"What're you doing!" I cry out. "You're gonna start the house on fire."

"No, just these photos," he mutters as smoke begins to funnel from the trunk.

I rush over to try to put the fire out as flames hiss from inside the trunk, but my dad sticks his arm out and pushes me back.

"Don't," he warns. "This needs to be done."

Micha is suddenly by my side and is shoving my dad away from me. "Don't ever fucking put your hand on her," he warns in a low, cold tone I've never heard him use before.

Then he grabs my hand and pulls me toward the stairway.

"What're you doing?" I hiss, trying to yank my hand away from his. "I want answers."

He shakes his head as he pulls me up the stairway. "Not like this. He's hungover and being an asshole, and I'm not just going to let him push you around like that. We'll get your stuff, stay at my house, and come back and talk to him later, when—and if—he gets sober."

"What about Lila?"

"She can stay at my house too. Ethan was already planning to anyway."

"Your mom's okay with that?"

"You know she is."

He's right. Micha's mom is the nicest person and has been there for me more than my own parents have.

"Okay." Right before we reach my room where Lila is, I stop him. I need to stay something—something important. "Micha, I think my dad may have just destroyed evidence."

He tucks a strand of my hair behind my ear and lets his hand linger on my cheek. "I know."

"And it was evidence the stalkers saw," I press.

"I know," he replies. "But pretty girl, this isn't really our problem. Whatever your mom and dad did, that's their problem. Not yours." He looks me straight in the eye. "And I need to be sure you understand that."

I nod. "I do, but—"

"No buts," he cuts me off. "I don't want you worrying about this. Ryder is looking into the stalker. Your dad can handle whatever the fuck we just witnessed happen in the living room. And you and I are just gonna relax for the week while everything gets handled, okay?"

"You're being so bossy," I mutter.

He cracks a small smile. "I know, and I'm not a fan of it, but right now, I think it needs to happen or else you're going to get caught up in whatever mess your parents got themselves into. And I don't want that to happen. I want to protect you. That's my job as your husband and best friend."

I nod, pretending like I fully agree with him, but the thing is, I may have gotten mixed up in this a long time ago. Back when it all happened. I had never told Micha, but the first time the police investigated my mom, I had tried to figure out what was going on, my teenage brain stupidly believing I could actually solve the murder and prove her innocence. Of course, I never did, although at one point I believed I did. And ever since then, I've always wondered how my mom had gotten mixed up in all of this. It was a mystery left unsolved, and while Micha may want me to stay out of it now, I'm not sure I can.

ELLA

LILA and I end up taking our bags over to Micha's house. My dad wanders off to God knows where, but considering the trunk was missing when we got back downstairs, I have a weird feeling he may have gone to either burn the entire trunk or bury it. Probably the latter, since I know my dad has a knack for burying things.

Just thinking about it reminds me of that night. That stupid night that I never think about, and haven't had to, except for now.

"I forgot something in my room," I tell Micha the moment we step into his house.

I set the bag down onto the floor and turn to leave, but his fingers circle around my arm, stopping me.

"You want me to go with you?" he asks.

I shake my head. "I just forgot my shampoo. I think I left it in the shower." When he makes no effort to let me go, worry creasing his pretty features, I add, "Micha, my dad isn't at the house any more, and I'm going to be over there for like three minutes tops. I'll be fine." I hate lying to him, and I plan on telling him the truth, but when we're in private.

He reluctantly lets me go. "If you're not back in five minutes, I'm coming over to look for you."

I roll my eyes but kiss his cheek, then rush out the door. Heavy snowfall is tumbling from the sky and scattering across the ground as I jog across the yard, hop over the fence, and hurry inside the house. With how cloudy the sky is and the amount of snowfall, I'm betting a blizzard is rolling in, which means if Ethan doesn't get here quickly, he'll get snowed out. Knowing Ethan, though, he's probably prepared for that type of situation—he's weird like that.

But anyway, as I hurry into my house, the stench of burnt photos, stale cigarettes, and booze lacing the air, I decide maybe a blizzard might not be bad since it'll keep the creepy stalker from paying a visit to Star Grove. At least for now. And it'll slow down the detectives working my mom's case. Because while I may have always forced myself to believe my mom was innocent, watching my dad burn those photos has me questioning things. Not if my mom was guilty, but if my dad was. It's something I've always wondered since I saw him burying this in the backyard all those years ago. I'd unburied it for who knows what reason—curiosity probably—and then tucked it away under my floorboards.

The floorboard I'm currently crouched over. I pry the board out, stick my hand into the hole, and pull out the object I saw my dad burying late one night after the police had stopped by asking questions about a man whose body hadn't turned up yet, but would later on. His name was Harold Mapleton, and his body was found in the mountains late one night, frozen in one of the many rivers that thread the town of Star Grove. And on that very same night, I saw my dad bury this in our backyard in the middle of the night. He had to work really hard to dig a hole too— the ground was so frozen, so it must've been important to bury the key. Maybe he was just being drunk and weird—that was sort of my dad's MO. But I don't know, even to this day it's bothered me. Not that there's an actual connection between the murder to the key and the body, and I have no idea what the key goes to or why I felt compelled to keep it. And for the most part, I hardly ever thought about it. Now, though...

"I want to find out what this goes too," I mutter as I stare at the key.

I have no clue how to go about doing that, but with a bunch of free time on my hands, I can at least try to figure it out. I also think it might be time to figure out what really happened between my mom and Harold.

I just hope this ends the way I want it to. That my parents will be innocent.

The problem is they've rarely been innocent in anything they used to be involved in. That much I do know about them.

MICHA

ELLA'S KEEPING something from me—I know her well enough that I can tell. But that's okay for now since I'm keeping something from her.

"Hey, mom," I greet my mom in the kitchen after Ella heads back to her house to grab her shampoo, and Lila is grabbing her suitcase out of her car.

A smile lights up her face as she turns away from the stove and toward me. "Oh my God, why didn't you call me and tell me you were coming!" She wraps her arms around me and gives me a big hug.

"Sorry. It was kind of a sporadic decision," I say, hugging her back.

She pulls back to look me in the eye. "Is everything okay?"

I waver. "Kind of. I just had to leave the tour a little bit early."

"Are you and Ella doing okay?" she asks worriedly.

"Of course," I assure her. "We just needed a little bit of a break from the road."

"That's understandable," she says, turning back to the stove where she's cooking what looks like eggs. "Why'd you guys drive here separately, though? It seems a bit strange. Are you sure everything's okay?"

"Yeah, everything's fine, Mom. I promise," I say, but my phone vibrates from inside my pocket, reminding me of all the shit going on right now.

That's probably Ryder with an update. The last one he gave me was during my drive over, and the information made me really uneasy. Ryder had basically told me that he'd looked at the hotel security footage and discovered it was a man and woman that were stalking me, which I guess I sort of already assumed. However, it still made me nervous when he confirmed it, that there are two people stalking me and that Ryder had actually seen them on the footage following me around. I had planned on telling Ella what I found out once I got to her house, but then her father lit those photos on fire, and I decided to keep this to myself for now, not wanting to add to her stress.

"Hold on, I gotta take this call," I tell my mom then

wander back to my room for some privacy. Then I dig out my phone and answer, "Hey."

"Hey, it's Ryder," he says. "I have an update on the car they're driving. I can give you the make and model so you can keep an eye out. It's a blue Toyota Camry. I saw them getting into it from the security footage outside of the hotel."

"That's a pretty typical car."

"I know. But you can at least keep an eye out."

"Okay, thanks."

"I'm looking into a couple of leads. I'll call you tonight with an update."

"Thanks."

We hang up, and I feel the heaviness of the situation weighing onto my shoulder. Even worse, when I look outside, I see a blue car driving down the road. Although, I can't make out the model of the vehicle. Plus, logically, there's no way they could've driven all the way here if they were just at the hotel this morning. Still, goosebumps sprout across my arms, knowing whoever they are, they've been to Star Grove before. How else would they have gotten a hold of that trunk with the photos?

Also, another thing that's really, really bothering me, is why they chose to throw that trunk at me, almost as if they knew seeing those photos would freak me out.

Almost as if they knew Ella's mom is a suspect in a cold case linked to Harold Mapleton. But if that's the case, then what's the real reason behind everything they're doing?

That's what I need to find out. I just hope the answers come soon before these people end up showing up in Star Grove.

ABOUT THE AUTHOR

Jessica Sorensen is a *New York Times* and *USA Today* bestselling author who lives in the snowy mountains of Wyoming. When she's not writing, she spends her time reading and hanging out with her family.

For information: jessicasorensen.com

Enchanted Chaos

Shimmering Chaos

Untitled (coming soon)

Capturing Magic:

Chasing Wishes

Chasing Magic

Untitled (coming soon)

Chasing Hadley Harlyton:

Chasing Hadley

Falling for Hadley

Holding onto Hadley

Untitled (coming soon)

Tangled Realms:

Forever Violet

Untitled (coming soon)

Curse of the Vampire Queen:

Tempting Raven

Enchanting Raven

Alluring Raven

Untitled (coming soon)

The Illusion Series:

The Unraveling of Lies

Untitled (coming soon)

Rules of Willow & Beck:

Rules of Willow & Beck

Untitled (coming soon)

The Heartbreaker Society:

The Liar

Untitled (coming soon)

Guardian Academy Series:

Entranced

Entangled

Enchanted

The Forest of Shadow & Bone

Entice

Charmed

Untitled (coming soon)

Sunnyvale Series:

The Year I Became Isabella Anders

The Year of Falling in Love

The Year of Second Chances

Untitled (coming soon)

The Coincidence Series:

The Coincidence of Callie and Kayden

The Redemption of Callie and Kayden

The Destiny of Violet and Luke

The Probability of Violet and Luke

The Certainty of Violet and Luke

The Resolution of Callie and Kayden

Seth & Greyson

The Evermore of Callie & Kayden

Untitled (coming soon)

The Shattered Promises Series:

Shattered Promises

Fractured Souls

Unbroken

Broken Visions

Scattered Ashes

Breaking Nova Series:

Breaking Nova

Saving Quinton

Delilah: The Making of Red

Nova and Quinton: No Regrets

Tristan: Finding Hope

Wreck Me

Ruin Me

Untitled (coming soon)

The Fallen Star Series:

The Fallen Star

The Underworld

The Vision

The Promise

The Lost Soul

The Evanescence

The Mist of Starts (coming soon)

The Darkness Falls Series:

Darkness Falls

Darkness Breaks

Darkness Fades

The Death Collectors Series (NA and YA):

Ember X and Ember

Cinder X and Cinder

Spark X and Spark

Unbeautiful Series:

Unbeautiful

Untamed

CPSIA information can be obtained
at www.ICGtesting.com
Printed in the USA
LVHW091457110122
708305LV00006B/420